WAITING FOR A STAR TO FALL

Lucy and Ethan grew up together. Lucy worshipped Ethan from afar and was disenchanted when he left for university, and didn't return. She hadn't realised that this was because of his family's hidden problems. Lucy is now the village librarian and Ethan is a well-known author. When Ethan comes back to the village and into her life again, can he shed his obsession with the past? Will they master the obstacles and find each other before it's too late?

WENDY KREMER

WAITING FOR A STAR TO FALL

Complete and Unabridged

LINFORD
Leicester

First published in Great Britain in 2009

First Linford Edition
published 2011

British Library CIP Data

Kremer, Wendy.
    Waiting for a star to fall. - -
    (Linford romance library)
    1. Women librarians- -Fiction. 2. Authors
    - -Fiction. 3. Love stories.
    4. Large type books.
    I. Title II. Series
    823.9′2–dc22

    ISBN 978–1–44480–528–4

Published by
F. A. Thorpe (Publishing)
Anstey, Leicestershire

Set by Words & Graphics Ltd.
Anstey, Leicestershire
Printed and bound in Great Britain by
T. J. International Ltd., Padstow, Cornwall

This book is printed on acid-free paper

1

Lucy followed the back of the man's head with her eyes as he walked down the room. His thick dark hair was neatly cut and brushed the collar of his Barbour jacket. He went towards the reference section and turned the corner; his face still hidden. There was an air of isolation about his tall figure.

Her breath caught in her throat, her pulse escalated. It must be a figment of her imagination — even if it was Ethan, he didn't mean anything to her anymore — he'd been gone too long. She looked at the large wall clock opposite and waited patiently for the last stragglers to present their books.

When he reached the desk, he put down a book entitled, *Perfect Crimes*. The library card was new. Lynne must have issued it when she was out. She scanned the book without looking up at him.

He leaned forward slightly and smiled. 'Hello, Lucy! Mum told me you were working here now. How do you like it?'

A knot rose in her throat. She handed him his card. 'Hello, Ethan! Very much! Back for a longer stay? You haven't needed a library card before.'

His eyes swept her face approvingly. He had a set of blue eyes that had always made female hearts flutter. 'I'm here for a couple of days at least.' His brows crinkled questioningly. 'How long since we last met?'

She pushed the book across the desk. 'Almost ten years, I should think.'

His expression was intent, appraising; he whistled softly. 'Well, I must say you've changed for the better.' He tilted his head and smiled at her.

It was an effort not to return his smile. She shuffled papers into a neat pile and waited.

'I called to see Colin last night, and met Judy. It was almost like old times.'

Her throat was dry and she found it

difficult not to sound resentful. 'Really?'

He studied her face; there was delicacy and strength in her features. He said, 'Colin was, and still is, the best friend I ever had.' She remained silent. He was too intelligent not to feel her censure and added, 'I didn't forget him, Lucy. I was busy and I'm not a good letter writer.'

It slipped out promptly. 'Coming from a best-selling author, that's nonsensical.'

His lips tightened; there was a pause. His reply when it came surprised her. 'You're right. I should have made an effort. I wasn't such a good friend, after all, was I?'

Colour flooded her cheeks. She instantly regretted her remark. He gave her no chance to soften its effect. He picked up his book and went towards the door. A blast of cold air rushed in as he went out.

Walking along rain-drenched pavements and looking down at the reflection of streetlamps on the surface, Ethan was deep in thought. Lucy had trailed after

Colin and him like a limpet until she was in grammar school.

The poised young woman behind the desk was a pleasant contrast to the spindle-legged teenager with unruly hair. Lost in memories of the past, he increased his pace and mused she was right — it wouldn't have cost him much effort to keep in touch.

A short time later, Lucy bundled her slender body into her ankle-length red wool coat and locked the library door. She thought about Ethan; she'd been hopelessly in love with him when she was a teenager.

At home, there was a delicious smell drifting down the hallway from the kitchen.

'Lucy? Come and see who's here!'

Her breath caught in her throat; she knew it would be Ethan before she entered the room, and it was. He was sitting at the large farmhouse table.

Her mother was fairly short with a quiet oval face. Laughter lines creased her features when she quickly explained.

'I met Ethan down the village. His mother is out visiting Mrs Alden — she's ill in bed, so I invited him for a meal. Aren't you going to say hello?'

Ethan intervened. 'We've met already, earlier on.'

'Oh, and I thought I'd surprise her!' Disappointed, Mrs Waring tried to hurry things along. 'The food is all ready; we're just waiting for you, love.'

'Carry on! I'll wash my hands first.' As she did, out of the corner of her eye, she watched Ethan filling his plate. Lucy sat down and warmth returned to her body. She tried to adjust to his presence and ate determinedly. Seeing him there, the years rolled backwards.

Her father fitted his broad back more comfortably into the form of the kitchen chair and picked up the interrupted conversation. 'And people bought them?'

Ethan laughed softly. 'It surprised me too! I only started painting for fun, but a man with a small art gallery in Alicante said he could sell the pictures to tourists. He still does.'

'And you write books?'

'My main income comes from my books these days. I don't paint very much now; I don't have the time, but the art dealer will still take as many paintings as I give him.'

'I don't want to be critical but writing and painting aren't exactly secure jobs are they?'

It seemed that old habits die hard; Lucy rushed to his defence. 'Ethan writes bestsellers, Dad. Everyone agrees that his books are really good.'

Ethan watched her for a moment, resting his forearm on the edge of the tables and with his fork poised in the air. His mouth curved into an unconscious smile as he said, 'I'd have stayed in the bank if all I wanted was security; but I know what you mean. I always invest some of the money I get; who knows how long I'll sell books, or paintings?'

Mr Waring looked out from under bushy eyebrows. 'To be honest, everyone thought you'd end up in your father's bank.'

'My father did too. I don't think he ever understood why I wanted to go to university.'

'Well . . . I'm sure your mum's delighted to have you home now.' Lucy's mother pushed second helpings in his direction.

'Umm! I came because she's had a terrible cough for ages and she just seems to ignore it. I hope to take her back to Spain with me for a while. I've tried to persuade her over the phone, but it's no good; I decided I have to pressure her personally.'

Her mother nodded. 'Good idea! She buys too much cough mixture over the counter. I keep on telling her to go to the doctor's, but she won't listen.'

Ethan's blue eyes twinkled. 'I'm hoping a change of scenery and a short holiday will do the job and clear things up. It's not very warm in Spain at the moment, but it's a darned sight milder than it is here.'

Lucy's father laughed cheerfully. 'Well, that's true, no doubt, and that house isn't the most congenial place to be at this time of year either.'

Ethan ran his fingers through his thick curly hair; it gleamed in the overhead lighting and sprang back obediently into place. 'To be honest I didn't realise the house was in such bad shape. Quite honestly it's much too big for her — with all those empty bedrooms upstairs, and the unused rooms downstairs.'

'We all thought she'd downsize when your father died.'

Ethan shook his head. 'She loves the place, even if it is a rambling liability, but it needs modernising; even she admits that now. She just can't face organising everything.'

Lucy's mother mused, 'Well, she's on her own, and not so young any more, but I understand why she's fond of the house. After a time a house becomes part of you. We've lived in this one for thirty years.'

Ethan laid his cutlery aside and folded his arms behind his head; the back of the chair creaked. The sleeves of his twill shirt were rolled up to the elbow and the rich outlines of his shoulders strained against the fabric. He looked around. 'This house was always like a second home to me.'

Lucy rose from her chair to collect the dirty dishes.

Her mother beamed, 'Yes, they were good times, weren't they, when you were kids? And thank heavens, none of you ever got into really serious trouble, did you?'

Lucy was thinking about their childhood too. Her mother put a trifle on the table and handed Ethan a large spoon. Lucy turned towards the sink and ran the hot water. 'Not for me, thanks!'

Her father's voice went on. 'How long are you planning to stay, Ethan?'

Ethan swung his head around to look at Lucy busy with the dishes, and then back again. She was barely as high as his shoulder, pleasantly slender without being thin. He replied, 'It depends. If I can persuade Mum, we'll be off as soon

9

as she packs her bags.'

For once, Lucy was glad to do the washing up. The conversation purred behind her back. Her parents brought him up to date about people he knew, and local news. Lucy didn't join in. She was annoyed that his nearness still disturbed her so much. She groped around in her mind for negative thoughts to dampen the traces of exhilaration she felt . . . if he'd visited his mother more often and stayed longer when he came he would have noticed the house needed attention a long time ago.

His stays were rare and brief, although she'd heard all about them afterwards, from his mother. He didn't even attend his father's funeral. They hadn't been able to contact him; he'd been hiking around Australia at the time.

On her way to a Saturday appointment her mother handed her a plastic carrier-bag. 'Drop this off at Susan's on the way, Lucy. I borrowed some cake tins the last time I filled the freezer. She's sure to want to do some baking now, for Ethan.'

Lucy sighed resignedly. She didn't really mind the errand, but she didn't want to bump into Ethan. He awakened too many conflicting emotions when she saw him. It was peaceful as she walked up the curved drive to the rambling detached house. She rang the bell and waited impatiently in the tiled porch. After a minute, she bent to put the bag in front of the door, but heard the sound of approaching foot-steps. It opened suddenly.

Looking up the length of his long legs in washed-out jeans, past the blue and white check shirt, her glance rested on his face. His eyes were hauntingly blue. He was now the centre of local interest; a home-grown celebrity. 'Is your mother in? Mine asked me to return these baking tins.'

His cheek creased, and he smiled. 'You've just missed her, she's shopping. Come in!'

'No, thanks, I'm on my way to the hairdresser.'

He smiled knowingly. 'I suppose that's as good an excuse as any.' Their eyes locked.

She formed her lips into a stiff smile and felt rattled. 'It's not an excuse; it's the truth. Just because you're a local celebrity doesn't mean I need to join the admiration society does it?'

He looked at her lazily through half-closed lids. 'Pity!' Suddenly he put one hand each side of her head, against the decorative Victorian tiles on the wall, and leaned forward. The smell of sandalwood was strong and heady. His face was too close for comfort.

Lucy ducked neatly under his arm. 'You're conceited, Ethan, and you vastly overestimate your attractions. You may impress others, but not me!'

'Who's trying to impress anyone? You're getting het up about nothing, and misinterpreting a quite innocent invitation! I was just being polite that's all. Scared?'

Lucy thought she could detect laughter in his eyes, and that irritated her even more. His square shaped face was close and much too familiar. She hid her confusion. 'Huh! Scared indeed! You and Colin drove me mad when we were kids and I've no intention of jumping through your hoop any more. I'm grown up and independent now — in case you haven't noticed!'

He hooted with laughter. 'We did what? Do I have to remind you, you were the one who drove us crazy when you trailed after us from the time you could walk, until the third form!'

She thrust the plastic bag at him and turned away, without further comment.

His voice drifted after her. 'I'll tell Mum you called.'

She knew he was still watching. Lucy's pulse pounded as she marched away; she hated the fact he still managed to make her feel like a gauche and unsophisticated teenager.

She called at her brother's next day. Judy and Colin's house was at the other end of the village. Her nephew, Tim, was busy with a red plastic tractor. 'Where's Colin?'

'He's helping Ethan to clear the wilderness at 'The Vicarage'.'

Lucy's brows rose in surprise.

'He came to ask Colin if he knew where he could borrow a chainsaw, so Colin gave him his, and offered to help. They were the best of friends once, weren't they?'

'Yes. Ethan was always there. I can't remember a time when he wasn't.' She turned to open her arms to her nephew, toddling determinedly towards her. 'I came to ask if you'd like me to take Tim off your hands for a while. I'll take him to the playground.'

'Umm, that would be great; give me time to clean the kitchen! Coming to the bonfire?'

'If I can get there on time. What times does it start?'

'As soon as it gets dark I expect. Ethan and Colin are adding what they cut this morning to the pile.'

It was damp underfoot in the field behind the church; the big fire was already burning brightly when Lucy arrived. She searched for her sister-in-law and found her among the throng of people nearest the fire. Tim's eyes were round like saucers. To her surprise, Ethan was there too, on the other side of the fire.

Watching him was like someone prodding sharply in an old wound. When they were young, Ethan had been her idol. He was Colin's best friend; almost a second brother. She followed them round like a lapdog, until she developed a crush on Ethan and began to feel tongue-tied and blush a lot in his presence. She then moved away, began to watch him from a distance.

She saw him get top results in his exams, was always envious if she saw him with a girlfriend, and finally learned to concentrate on other things.

With a bundle of excellent A-Levels in his pocket he'd left for university and seldom come home again afterwards.

Lucy focused her energies on her own schoolwork to hide the feeling of loss, and eventually she decided to become a librarian.

★ ★ ★

'Morning, Lucy!'

She looked up and smiled. 'Hello, Mrs M. finished your books already?'

'No not quite; the one you gave me about Mary Stuart is very good. I'm only popping in to say hello.' Ethan's mother looked frail. Her skin was white and drawn tightly over her cheeks; her blue eyes were almost too tight.

'Is your cough better?'

The older woman sounded a little annoyed. 'Now don't you start as well! Ethan keeps on all the time. He wants me to go back to Spain with him, when he goes.'

Lucy smiled. 'That's a very sensible idea.'

'I'm thinking about it. I won't be pushed!'

Lucy nodded. She had plenty of friends her own age, but Susan Mason had always been an important part of her life. She was like a favourite aunt. At first, Lucy kept in touch because she was thirsty for information about Ethan and later simply because she liked her.

'By the way, have you finished the John Grisham book yet, by any chance? I told you someone has put it on the request list, didn't I?'

Her hand flew to her mouth. 'Oh yes! I meant to bring it. It's on my bedside table.'

'Don't worry! If you don't mind, I'll pick it up this evening.'

'No, of course not. Fetch it by all means.'

'I'll call in on the way home.'

'There's a Women's Institute meeting at six, but Ethan will be at home.'

★ ★ ★

A diffused haze shone through the pattern of coloured glass; it helped to

17

light up the darkness as she stood in the porch. It was cold in the shelter of the covered entrance, and she pulled her scarf more tightly around her throat. Ethan opened the door.

'Hi, there! What an unexpected pleasure! Come in!' She followed the sweeping gesture of his hand, waited until he closed the door, and then she followed him as he walked down the long hallway towards the living room.

'I'm here to pick up a library book from your mother.'

'She's not here, but she said you might call.'

Lucy's cheeks were pink from the cold. Looking at her eager greenish eyes, auburn hair, and generous lips, Ethan reflected that she was an extremely attractive young woman. He opened the door and stood aside to let her pass.

'Could you get it for . . . ?' Her voice trailed to a standstill when she saw another woman sitting comfortably in an easy chair next to the fire; the

18

shadow of the flames flittered across her face and settled in the folds of her crimson sweater. Lucy felt twinges of resentment, and tried quickly to disguise them. 'Oh, I'm sorry. I won't interrupt. I'll call another time.'

'Don't be silly.' He motioned towards the settee. 'Do you know Rachael?'

'No, but pleased to meet you!'

Ethan put a hand in his pocket. 'Rachael is a new partner with Wilbey and Boss, the solicitors in Drayton; she specialises in contractual law. Rachael, this is Lucy.'

Rachael smiled politely in Lucy's direction. 'Hello!'

He moved to the sideboard. 'Here Lucy, have something to keep out the cold.'

He handed her a long stemmed glass with amber liquid swirling invitingly in its depths. Lucy removed her gloves hurriedly, stuffed them into her pockets, and took the glass.

'Give me your coat, and sit down.'

'Thanks, but I won't stop. If you'll

get me the book I'll be off.'

'I'll get it.' He left the room, and suddenly it seemed very empty.

The two women were silent. Lucy sat gingerly on the edge of the seat. She looked at Rachael; she was pretty. Rachael's hands played with her glass. Lucy held hers tightly, and she jumped when Rachael asked.

'What do you do?'

Lucy took a sip of golden sherry; it tasted sweet and aromatic. 'I'm a librarian.'

'Here in the village?'

'Yes.' Lucy paused, and then said politely. 'Wilbey and Boss have a good reputation.'

'Yes, it's an excellent, solid firm. Ethan was looking for someone who could check a contract for any loopholes, and he found our address via the internet. I don't normally visit clients at home but he's a very persuasive man, isn't he? I made an exception.'

Lucy was silent. She studied the stencilled frieze of rambling roses and the mirror above the fireplace. She was annoyed with herself for feeling glad that Rachael wasn't Ethan's girlfriend.

'You live locally?'

The question made her jump again. 'Yes, I've lived here nearly all my life. I went away to train in a city library and I enjoyed that, but I wasn't sorry to come back. I live at home, with my parents.'

Rachael's long fingers with their crimson nails stroked the stem of her glass. 'How long have you known Ethan?'

'All my life. He's my brother's best friend. He practically lived in our house when we were kids . . . ' Lucy broke off as Ethan came in with the book in his hands.

She took the book, and plonked the glass down on the nearest table.

'Bye Lucy!' His voice floated down the hallway after her as she slammed the door and the old fashioned knocker rattled a little as she hurried down the driveway.

21

2

Mrs Mason had phoned and asked Lucy to call. Lucy now sat expectantly in the easy chair next to the fire. The floor-length windows were framed with yellow, pink and white chintz curtains. The colours were mirrored in an oil painting of extravagant full-blown cabbage roses above the long sideboard. She wondered where Ethan was, but was determined not to ask.

'Had a busy day?' Susan Mason put a tray on the coffee table and sat down.

'Quite busy; lots of schoolchildren stocking up on books today.'

'Well, they're better off reading than watching TV, or playing computer games.'

Lucy nodded. 'I agree! So . . . why did you want to see me?'

Mrs Mason poured them tea. 'You haven't been on holiday yet have you?'

Regarding her with curiosity, Lucy replied. 'No.'

'You can get time off whenever you like?'

Lucy nodded. 'More or less.'

'Good. You see I wondered if you'd come to Spain with me?'

Lucy was startled. 'I . . . I thought you were going with Ethan?'

'I am, but once I'm settled, he has to go back to London to clear up some things with his publisher. Perhaps I'm just being selfish, but I'd like to have someone else I know with me, and I thought you might enjoy a visit to Spain. I'm staying with him until after Christmas.

'Why not just wait until Ethan has finished his business, and go with him then?'

She replied impatiently. 'He's driving me mad, that's why! He insists I go now because of my cold; if I won't, he'll drag me to a specialist!'

Lucy chuckled. 'Is the idea of a visit to a doctor so daunting?'

'No, of course not, but they'll only prescribe a different cough mixture, tell me to wrap up and keep warm, and give me another appointment for the following week!'

'You shouldn't make light of it; you've had your cough for too long and it sounds worse every day.' She paused. 'Does Ethan know?'

'That I want you to come? Of course he does. I wouldn't invite anyone without his approval. What do you say?'

The suggestion was tempting; a relaxing holiday abroad with nothing special to do. She got on well with Mrs Mason. 'Hmm . . . '

'Oh, do come, Lucy! We'll enjoy ourselves. I know it might be more fun for you with someone younger, but most of your friends have already been away, haven't they?'

'Yes, they have.' Lucy was testing the idea. 'It's kind of you Mrs M. Are you sure?'

Mrs Mason looked hopeful. 'I'd simply love it. Think about it; and let me know.'

Two days later after lunch, she

walked up the drive again and spotted Ethan busy cutting back bushes. She'd almost, but not quite, adjusted to seeing his face again. Now that she'd absorbed his return and spoken with him a couple of times, she also felt the return of the kind of camaraderie they'd always shared.

He stopped, pulled off his thick gardening gloves, cast her neat figure in a smart grey and caramel winter costume an approving glance, and then gave her an arresting smile.

The surge of emotion that it triggered floored her a little, but she vowed she wasn't going to tumble headlong for him again. She was a sensible grown up woman now; she had things under control. 'I'm surprised to see you so busy in the garden. What about your book?'

He studied her thoughtfully and slapped the gloves across his palm. 'I'm working out ideas in my head and hacking at the undergrowth at the same time. It's therapeutic. Fancy some coffee? Or have you another hairdresser's appointment?'

She grinned. 'I'm on my way to work. Some of us do have to work for a living!' She glanced at her wristwatch. 'I've a couple of minutes if you're making coffee, but I came to see your mum. Is she in?'

'She'll be back any minute. She's only gone to the postbox.'

Lucy followed him down the hall into the kitchen. She noticed that even though the radiators were giving off some heat, the house was too cold for this time of year. She wasn't surprised his mother had a persistent cold. She stopped short in her silent criticism; he intended to get things modernised — he'd said so, and Ethan always kept to his word.

'What would you like, coffee or tea?'

'Coffee, please.' She cleared her throat. 'Your mother has invited me to Spain.'

He filled the kettle and nodded. 'It's a good idea.'

'You don't mind?'

He looked unconcerned. 'No, why should I? My mother obviously likes you. I expect she's explained I have urgent business in London, and I want her out of this house as soon as I can. When I'm finished in London, I'll come home again to check on the improvements. If she's away for a few weeks it'll give me an ideal opportunity to get the essentials sorted out. The central heating is outdated and the place needs new windows and a new front door. I'm sure she'll feel a lot happier in Spain with someone she knows around if I'm not there, so if you think you'd enjoy yourself . . . '

She said firmly. 'I wouldn't want to intrude on your privacy.'

His voice was insistent. 'If I didn't want you there, I'd say so.'

'As long as you're really sure? Don't forget to tell me how much my ticket and a rental car cost, so that I can refund the money. It would be easier if you organise them, please!'

He lifted his shoulder slightly but didn't argue. 'Good. I'll book everything.' There was a short pause. 'You get on with Mum well, don't you?'

'It's not difficult to get on with your mother, she's not demanding.'

His smile flashed, and he said, 'Was that meant to infer I am?'

She was startled. 'No such thing. We've both grown up and changed. I can't pass judgment because I don't know you well enough anymore.'

He watched her carefully. 'Do you realise she expected us to fall in love, and produce several grandchildren?'

Her face flamed. 'What! Why did she believe that?'

Stroking his chin, he regarded her carefully. 'Perhaps she remembers you had a crush on me once, and as I've not shown any sign of settling down with anyone else, she probably still lives in hope.'

She was lost for words and highly embarrassed. 'A crush? On you? What nonsense!'

'Aw! Come off it! You used to shadow us all the time. Colin told me it was because you were potty about me; and he said so when my mum was around! It appalled me at the time, I can tell you. I must have been roughly sixteen or seventeen!'

Heatedly, she fenced again. 'Well, you were misinformed! Wait till I get my hands on my brother. I can see now why you write books; you're very good at making things up.'

He grinned and sounded innocent when he said, 'I didn't make it up; your own brother, Colin, told me so.'

She was almost in control again. 'You're insufferable.' Even though Lucy had secretly vowed not to quiz him, it slipped out. She was glad to re-direct their conversation. 'Why didn't you come home more often, and stay longer?'

His expression steadied. 'I don't have the good memories of this house that Mum has.'

'You have bad memories?'

His voice had a steely edge. 'Not of

29

the house, of my father . . . we didn't get on.'

Lucy was surprised by the turn the conversation had taken. 'Yes, I noticed that. You were very reserved with each other, weren't you? But lots of teenagers go through a thorny patch with their parents when they're growing up. I thought it was a passing thing.'

His hands slid out of his pockets and he turned to fiddle with a fruit-bowl on the table. He shrugged. 'Just one of those things. I started to lead my own life, and I knew Mum was all right, so it wasn't really important.'

★   ★   ★

Ethan called at the library on Monday morning. 'I'm off to book our tickets. Will next Saturday morning be all right with you?'

'Fine!'

'Good. Oh, your mum has invited me for a meal again; I'll give you the details then.'

'I'll see you, but not for long — I'm going out.'

He hesitated, blinking. 'Ah! A date?'

'It's none of your business, but yes.'

He didn't understand why he felt uptight, but he had to plough on. 'Do I know him?'

'No. I don't think so. His name is Lance Parfitt. He's an accountant.'

'Known him long?'

'Long enough . . . stop questioning me Ethan! I'm a big girl now.'

He thrust his hands firmly into his pockets. 'See you later then?'

After the meal he thanked her mother and offered Lucy a lift. 'Where are you meeting him?'

'Outside the new cinema.' Surprised she asked. 'You have a car?'

'I hired one. I need to visit companies to fix up about the house alterations.'

They sat lulled in the cocoon of the car, listening to radio music. A few minutes later he pulled smoothly into the kerb.

'Thanks for the lift.'

'Is he waiting?'

Briefly she recalled the time when Colin and Ethan had been her designated guards. She hoisted her shoulder bag and took a quick look. 'Over there, by the entrance.'

'Hmm! Why didn't he come to pick you up?'

She gave an audible sigh. 'He was out with a client. We agreed to meet here.'

'How will you get home?'

'He has a car too. Stop the cross-examination, I want to get out.'

Watching her meet the unknown man, Ethan ran his hand over his face impatiently. What was wrong with him? He'd made a vow not to tease or to interfere but it was hard to forget the role he'd played when she was small, and he still wanted to protect her.

Ethan didn't see her again for a couple of days, but he heard all about what she'd been doing in the intervening years. He just casually mentioned her name, and his mother filled in the gaps. He next met Lucy one morning on his way to the newsagents. The beginning of a smile touched the corners of his mouth. 'Hi! Where are you off to? Running out of books?'

Blustery winds blew her hair about and she tried to brush it out of her face as she replied. 'That'll be the day! I'm on the way to the bank, to pay a bill.'

'Looking forward to the weekend?'

The cold wind brought colour to her cheeks. 'Of course! Counting the hours!'

He smiled at her enthusiasm. 'Hope you won't be disappointed.'

'What could be nicer than going on holiday to Spain with someone I like?'

He gave her a lop-sided grin. 'I didn't realise you were so fond of me.'

She wouldn't let him irritate her. She lifted her chin. 'I'm talking about your mother!'

He laughed. Recalling his intention, he suddenly felt unsure in her company — for almost the first time he could ever remember. The words came out in a rush. 'How about a pub meal tonight? Perhaps I can improve your opinion about me before we leave.'

'Oh!' He caught her completely off-guard. Feeling confused, she didn't know if she was glad or sorry that she had a real excuse. 'Thanks, but I already have a date, with Lance.'

Ethan shrugged and nodded. 'My loss is his gain.' He looked down at his watch. 'The bank closes in a couple of minutes. You'd better hurry!'

As he walked away, Ethan mused that perhaps it was better anyway. She was a straight down the line sort of girl, who wanted marriage and babies, definitely not his type at all.

* * *

Mrs Mason and Lucy sat next to their suitcases, while Ethan organised the rental-car. The journey to Heathrow and the flight to Spain had been uneventful. The information at the airport pouring out of the loudspeakers was foreign; Ethan's voice was more familiar, and she was glad when he interrupted her wanderings. He handed her driving licence back.

'I've rented it for a fortnight. You have to return the papers and keys here, to the same desk. I have my own jeep at home, but the gears are tricky, it's better for you to have a smaller car.'

His mother asked, 'How far is the villa from the airport?'

'About three-quarters of an hour.'

'Why did you come here in the first place?' Lucy asked.

He answered while concentrating on the sunlit road ahead. 'I visited the Costa Brava as a student and went inland to earn some money picking grapes. I liked the area and came back whenever I could. When someone told me this place was for sale I took out a loan, worked like a madman in various jobs to pay it off, and moved here.'

They were driving through open country, and through never-ending fields of vines. 'Do you grow grapes?'

He looked at her in the mirror and shook his head. 'I don't, but I join in at harvest time, when every extra pair of hands is welcome, and I also help with the paperwork for the local wine growers association whenever English is needed.'

Suddenly he turned off the main road on to a bumpy narrow track. Changing to a lower gear, the engine purred gratefully. The track sloped upwards towards a box-shaped building.

Mrs Mason leaned forward. 'So, this is it?'

'Yes. What do you think?' There was a hint of anticipation in his voice.

'Exactly like the photos. Quite lovely isn't it, Lucy?'

'Yes.' She considered the house and its background. 'It's a typical local farmhouse, isn't it?'

He nodded. 'The house was almost a ruin when I bought it. I've some photos of what it looked like before I did it up. Remind me to show you them.'

As they drew closer, Lucy saw that

the square building had solid white-washed walls. It stood overlooking fields of vines. The ground level had two storage rooms that stretched back into the darkness; one contained tools and machinery, and the other a black jeep. The car came to a halt. When she got out the air was cool and fresh. Lucy arched her back. 'What's all the machinery for? I thought you said you don't grow grapes?'

'I don't, but I rent my ground to a neighbour, and I let Antonio keep his tools here. I don't need the space, although I could turn them into extra rooms, if needed. Follow me; home is upstairs!'

Downstairs, adjacent to some steps leading upwards, was a rough table with a bench each side. It was beneath a pergola covered in rambling autumn vines. The steps led up to a large terrace with large ochre stone tiles. The view across the open valley was lovely. Never-ending lines of vines ran in lines down its sides.

Next morning, they decided to visit Barcelona. Ethan knew it well and it was a good idea to go there before he left. On arrival they strolled leisurely to some well-known tourist attractions and stopped for lunch in a typical Spanish restaurant. Heartened by the food and a glass of rich Spanish wine they went towards the cathedral.

Mrs Mason was determined to see the entire interior although she already looked overtired. Lucy and Ethan sat in the shadows at the back and waited; it wasn't necessary to make small talk. Lucy was content to sit with him in silence and look towards the high altar.

Lucy rose as Mrs Mason re-joined them. Ethan's hand brushed hers, and she had the urge to jump back. The tingling reaction made her wonder, despite all that she'd vowed, what she really felt about him. She stiffened and tilted her head pointedly at Mrs Mason as she met his glance and said, 'I've enjoyed it, but I think it was enough for one day. Unless one of you is determined to see more, I suggest that it's time we head for home.'

He'd picked up her signal. 'Agreed! I'll bring you back again one day. There's an awful lot more worth seeing, but too much is just as bad as too little. Ready, Mum?'

Mrs Mason nodded and looked almost relieved. When they got home they persuaded her to have a rest while they prepared a meal. They all dawdled over a glass of wine and talked about Barcelona.

Mrs Mason got up. 'I'm going to have an early night! I'm tired. Good night!'

Ethan and Lucy echoed goodnight and exchanged glances as a bout of coughing accompanied her down the corridor to her room. On their own, they caught up on each other's lives. Lucy enjoyed a cautious but genuine pleasure in his company. In the glow of the overhead lamp, and the sound of wood crackling in the fireplace, they played Scrabble and time passed in a flash.

Next morning Ethan had made coffee and was buttering his toast before Lucy arrived. He got up to get the coffee pot as she sat down opposite. She leaned back and sighed softly. 'This is just great.' He smiled and filled a coffee mug.

He gestured towards the table and the fridge. 'Help yourself! If you want a cooked breakfast, you'll find most things although I'm not sure about bacon.'

Lucy shook her head. 'No thanks!' She reached for the cornflakes. 'This is fine!'

They sat in amiable familiarity; it was filled with small talk about generalities and comments about the English news from the radio playing in the background. It was luxury for her to dawdle over breakfast and enjoy the treat of a second cup of coffee. He looked at his watch. 'Mum's late today! She's usually up before me.'

'She was tired last night. Let her sleep as long as she likes.'

He nodded. 'How about doing some shopping? We'll make plans when we get back.'

'Good idea.' Lucy was surprised how easily she was prepared to fall in with his ideas; it must be her holiday mood. You'd better leave a note for her, so she knows where we are.' She studied his face unhurriedly and liked what she saw.

'She won't be on her own for long. Maria comes in on Mondays.'

'Maria?'

'Antonio's wife; she looks after the housework for me.'

They strolled around the small supermarket in the nearby town and their trolley was soon full. When they drove home, it was almost midday. She leaned back. 'You always wanted to be your own boss, didn't you? In a sense, you are.' The car braked gently in a cloud of dust, to allow room for a passing tractor. He looked, shrugged and smiled. 'What about a wife and children?'

His answer was swift. 'Not for me; I'm not the marrying kind. I value my independence too much. I admire men like Colin who take on the responsibility, but I think life can be just as worthwhile if you consciously choose to live alone. I'd be miserable if I was tied down.'

Lucy shrugged. 'I suppose marriage isn't for everyone. You have to believe in it.'

He regarded her with curiosity. 'And you? Marriage, children?'

Tossing her head in a gesture of defiance, she said. 'Unlike you, I like the idea of marriage and a family.'

The idea of Lucy married with children knotted his stomach. 'Don't tell me you're considering marrying that puffed up accountant!'

'He's not puffed up!' She glared at him.

It shouldn't make any difference who she married, but it did. When they reached the house, the door opened and a short, dark-haired, plump woman rushed at them.

An incomprehensible machine-gun conversation followed. He looked shocked as he explained. 'Maria found Mum unconscious in the kitchen and called an ambulance.' 'I'm off to the hospital. You'll be all right on your own?'

'I want to come with you!' Dumping the bags at Maria's feet, they hurried back down the steps. 'The hospital is on the other side of the town.'

3

Lucy sat on a hard wooden chair, and wondered why none of them had realised just how ill Mrs Mason had been. Ethan was probably blaming himself, although if truth be told, it wasn't his fault. Mrs Mason had successfully hidden the true situation from everyone for too long. The sound of flapping doors heralded Ethan's re-appearance. She rose quickly. 'How . . . '

He looked tired and despondent. 'It could be heart disease or a chronic chest infection. She's medicated and sleeping. They'll stabilise her and do detailed tests. She seems to be reacting positively to antibiotics. At least it's not a heart attack, or a stroke.'

'Thank goodness for that!'

Lucy tried to find the right words to give him comfort. 'Well, it sounds encouraging. I'm sure they'd have told you if prospects were really bad.'

He nodded wordlessly and she fell in with him as they went towards the exit. He was silent and she decided to leave him to his own thoughts.

At home, he led the way towards the bedrooms, off a long narrow corridor that ran the length of the back of the house. Over his shoulder, he said, 'I'll pack a bag for her, and be off again.'

Next morning it took her a couple of seconds to adjust to her surroundings. Bright daylight streamed through the window and the simple white cotton curtains billowed in the breeze.

After a brief look out of the window at the slope of the hillside behind the house, she showered and dressed. Maria was busy at the sink.

Maria looked up. 'Ah, senorita! You have slept good.'

Lucy was pleased she could speak some English. 'Yes . . . yes very well, thank you. That coffee smells wonderful. Has Ethan phoned?'

Maria handed her a full mug. 'No, no

telephone. I come to listen how Mrs Mason is.'

Lucy's hands circled the china. 'No one knows what's wrong yet. Perhaps there's good news today.'

'Awful! Ethan always say she is good, kind mother.' Maria proceeded to fill a red plastic bucket with soapy water. 'I here, so I clean again, okay?'

'Yes . . . of course. Do whatever you like.'

Lucy took the coffee out on to the terrace. The parapet was cold and smooth as she leaned over it with her mug in her hand and looked across the valley. The sturdy vines stood in orderly rows like soldiers on parade. The earth was sienna brown, and the remnants of last year's leaves shivered in the wind.

Back inside, she found Maria was scrubbing the tiled floor in the living room. She looked up at Lucy and wiped her hands on her sensible apron. 'Antonio go to get supplies. You like to go too?'

Lucy brightened. The hired car was

downstairs but she didn't know where the keys were. Ethan was using his jeep. 'Yes, please. Can he drop me off by the hospital?'

Maria nodded. 'I tell him. He go soon.'

The medical staff had allowed her in, and hours later, Lucy was watching Mrs Mason sleeping. She stroked Mrs Mason's hand, lying on top of the white sheet. She was glad she'd come and managed to persuade Ethan to go home for a rest.

Early afternoon, on the way to the toilet, Lucy admitted she was worried; surely there should be some noticeable improvement by now? When she returned, she opened the door quietly and heard Mrs Mason's voice. It was weak, but clear.

'Of course I'm worried. If I die, you'll be all alone!'

'Don't be silly, Mum! You're not going to die.' Ethan looked up briefly from the bed towards the window to steady his expression.

Lucy waited for a moment. She knew how worried his mother was, that Ethan had no close relations. How could she reassure her? She walked quietly towards the other side of the bed and leaned down. 'Don't worry, he's got me. I'm there for him and he'll never be lonely or alone, promise. Ethan knows that, don't you, Ethan?'

Mrs Mason's eyes lit up, and two bright spots of colour shone on her pale cheeks. 'Ethan!' His mother's hand crept across towards him. Her voice was quiet but content. 'What good news; it's wonderful! I always dreamed of this happening; you know how much I like Lucy.'

Ethan looked stunned and Lucy was bewildered. Ethan opened his mouth, but his mother's voice was already fading as the latest dose of tranquillisers took effect. 'I wish I wasn't so tired. I want to hear all about how you two finally settled things . . . '

The door opened and the doctor entered, a nurse trailed behind him.

The consultant nodded briefly at them, and he said something in Spanish. Ethan got up.

Lucy was still staring at Mrs Mason wordlessly, her mouth slightly open. She was still swallowing the idea that Mrs Mason genuinely thought that she and Ethan were . . . She must be confused by the medication, and had misunderstood Lucy. Frozen like a block of salt, she suddenly realised Ethan was motioning impatiently for her to follow him outside. Lucy wondered if he'd see the funny side of it, but he didn't look amused.

'What on earth? Why did you say that?' His brows were drawn in an angry straight line.

Defensively she replied, 'I only wanted to reassure her. It was a quite innocent remark. She was the one who put two and two together and made five!'

The words ripped out of him impatiently. 'Of all the stupid . . . Do you realise she thinks we're together — or even that we're engaged?'

Her breath quickened and her cheeks were pink. 'She's always been worried about you ending up alone in the world. I wanted to help.' His eyes were bright but his expression wasn't at all pleased. The skin was tight on his cheek and Lucy knew he was angry, but she ploughed on anyway.

'Perhaps she won't remember a thing when she wakes up. Come on Ethan, it's not the end of the world, just a genuine mix-up! We'll clear it up later. Where's your sense of humour?'

'I fail to see the funny side of it! It's not funny!' He looked grim, glowered at her, and went on. 'Yes, she was drowsy, but she wasn't confused or mixed up. She won't forget.'

Her mood veered sharply to anger because of his reaction. 'Stop blaming me for everything! She misunderstood me. Go ahead, insist she understands what I meant next time she wakes up if you must. It'll upset her, but your momentary ego is clearly more important than her well-being.'

His voice was curt. 'I don't like lying to her or anyone else.'

Her breath burned in her throat. Her eyes darkened. 'You didn't lie, neither did I; she simply jumbled things up.'

The doctor and nurse came out and gave them some interested looks; their voices must have carried. He spoke briefly to Ethan before they went on their way. Ethan's jaw was tight and his expression was harsh. He turned and went back into the room.

Lucy stood stiffly, with clenched fists, bright eyes and pink cheeks for a minute or so then walked away, striding determinedly towards the exit. She knew part of the problem was because Ethan hated the idea of being tied to any woman. He was too unconventional and too independent to accept any kind of shackles. It was so stupid of him — when this particular problem could be easily disentangled.

Outside, she hoisted her bag to a more comfortable position and looked around. The small town was not on any tourist map; it had nothing special to recommend it. She headed for a small café and managed to order something to drink. The waiter brought her a fresh lemon drink which cooled her throat, and some of her anger.

She checked her money, and fished out a small phrase book from her bag. Her pronunciation was atrocious, but the waiter understood. A dilapidated taxi arrived and Lucy wrote Ethan's address on the back of a bill she found in her bag.

On arrival, he wrote down the fare on the same piece of paper. Pocketing the money and a generous tip, he gave her a smile. Lucy climbed the steps. The door wasn't locked: it always seemed to be open.

The phone rang and she ignored it. She started to prepare a meal. A short time later, she heard his jeep as it slithered to a stop and his feet echoing on the steps as he pounded upwards. When he reached the kitchen, she straightened. Jingling the key ring of the car in his hand, and said, 'Why didn't you wait? I intended to drive you home, after I'd checked my mother again.'

Staring at him quietly she replied, 'I'm not helpless.'

Ethan saw she was riled. His tone was almost apologetic. 'How did you get here? I was worried and phoned but no one answered.'

'I came by taxi. Not understanding Spanish, there wasn't much point in my answering the phone.' Lucy found she didn't enjoy being at odds with him. 'How's your mother?'

'They're optimistic. It's a serious chest infection. Antibiotics are working wonders.'

'Good! I'm really pleased!' He nodded, and Lucy gestured to the food. 'I've just made it. You're going back to the hospital?'

'Yes!' He took a look at the pan. 'I must admit I'm hungry and that looks good.'

'Then have some!' She put the pan with pasta and a thick tomato and meat sauce in the centre of the table and handed him the serving fork and spoon.

Ethan filled two glasses with wine and then filled his plate. Avoiding her glance, he said. 'She hasn't said much, but she did say she was delighted about our engagement.'

Lucy's fork stopped in mid-air and her eyes widened. 'Lord! So she really did misunderstand!'

'Yes, I know, it's crazy, and the mad thing about it is, I didn't have the heart to tell her the truth! I decided it was better to continue with the lie until she's better, like you said.'

Lucy forked a portion of the mixture into her mouth and chewed it slowly before she swallowed. 'Even though you are dying to put things right?'

'If she's starting to improve, I don't want to risk the slightest set-back.' His eyes watched her face. 'Do you mind continuing this farce for a little while, for her sake?'

She stared wordlessly across at him, her heart pounding. 'I don't want to get caught up in any romantic tomfoolery any more than you. As soon as she's fit we'll clarify things and I'm sure she'll laugh about it with us when we explain.'

He looked reflective. 'I wouldn't be so sure about that.' He reached out for his glass and took a sip. 'But we'll cross that bridge when we get to it.'

Lucy took a sip of wine too; it was smooth and had a subtle taste. She lifted her glass and asked. 'Is this local?'

'Probably from our fields outside; not bad is it?'

'We're drinking wine from your grapes?'

'Antonio mixes his grapes with the ones he grows here, so in a way it's mine.'

He looked at the oblong face of his metal wristwatch. 'I'd better get back.' He picked up the wine glass and lifted it in her direction. 'Thanks for the food, it was good.'

She touched her glass to his. 'To us and to your mum's recovery!'

He took a sip; the glass was still three-quarters full when he put it down. Ethan was glad they were back to normality again; for some reason he didn't like being at loggerheads with Lucy. 'Can I tell her that you'll be coming in tomorrow, if she asks?'

'Yes, of course. I'll stay with her; you can catch up on your sleep. Oh, where are the keys of the rental car?'

He smiled, picked up some keys from a nearby shelf, jingled them briefly and lifted his hand in silent farewell as he strode towards the door.

Mrs Mason did look much better. Her eyes had lost their lifeless expression, there was colour in her face again, and her voice was strong. She still had bouts of coughing, but even they didn't sound quite so aggressive, or last quite as long, any more. Ethan and Lucy stuck to their make-believe engagement and Lucy found it wasn't easy.

She was embarrassed by the idea and she had to be careful what she said. She hoped the charade would end soon.

Mrs Mason was still excited about what she believed was a genuine engagement.

'I'm so pleased.'

Lucy smiled uneasily and nodded.

'Have you been celebrating? Have you told your parents?'

Her mind floundered at the idea. 'Oh! . . . Well, no, we haven't. Not yet!'

'You must! Gosh, they're going to be surprised.'

Lucy's breath caught in her mouth. 'You can say that again!'

'I admit I was surprised too! Ethan hasn't been back long. You hadn't seen him for years and years.'

Two hours later, the doctor had made a visit, studied the charts and checked his patient. Mrs Mason began to stir again. Sleepily she asked. 'Lucy! How long have I slept this time?'

She chuckled. 'Two hours.'

Mrs Mason's eyes opened wide. 'That can't be true! What's the time?'

Lucy felt large hands on her shoulders; knew it was Ethan. He answered, 'It's three o'clock.' He leaned down and on impulse he kissed Lucy. Even though he was playing his part to perfection, Lucy worried whether it was necessary, or wise. His kiss was fleeting; his lips were warm and undemanding, but they still wakened unexpected desires.

'Back again? Slept well?' His mother smiled at him warmly.

He kissed her briefly on her forehead. 'I feel fine. I've slept . . . ' He looked briefly at his watch again. ' . . . Six, no nearly seven hours. How do you feel?'

'Better! Yes, a lot better.'

'The doctors are pleased with progress, but you'll have to stay in hospital until they're completely satisfied. Food is on the way. Soup I think.'

'That sounds wonderful. Take Lucy home Ethan! Please go and enjoy an evening together.'

4

Ethan was evidently feeling more like his old self again. Their cautious friendship was back on its old footing. It was cool in the evening, so Ethan usually lit a fire in the big open grate. The lighting was subdued; candles flickered on the mantelpiece and on side tables.

'Did I catch you unawares this afternoon?'

'This afternoon?'

'Kissing you . . . I thought we should play the part, for her sake.'

The colour rose in her face; she turned her head for a moment to readjust a plump cushion and hoped he hadn't noticed. 'I'm not sure that it was such a good idea, because things like that are bound to make things more complicated when the truth comes out.'

He looked thoughtful, circled the

wine in his glass, and said with tongue in cheek. 'I hadn't thought about that. To be honest I only felt nervous because we hadn't practiced!'

'Practiced? Are you kidding? From what your mother told me, practice is the last thing you need. I lost count of the female names she mentioned through the years.'

Startled, he said, 'Did she? She exaggerated, I'm sure.'

Her dark lashes framed knowing eyes. 'Don't pretend you've lived the life of a monk!'

'I don't, but I'm not the kind of Casanova you're making me to be either. I've met lots of nice girls; but kissing them, or kissing you, is a completely different kettle of fish.'

She couldn't stop herself. 'Is it? Why?'

He grinned. 'It's the difference between pleasure and friendship. I can't define it in words. It's just hard for me to feel passionate about you.'

'That's very flattering! Perhaps I

should say thanks? It's just as well that you don't bowl me over either.'

He laughed. It echoed through the room. 'That's the trouble, we know each other too well, and the chemistry won't work for us. By the way, have you phoned home yet?'

She was glad to be on safer ground. 'Not since we arrived. Funny, your mum asked me the same thing this afternoon. I've waited, so that I can tell them she is OK again.'

'Your parents are probably waiting to hear from you.'

'Yes, you're probably right. I'll phone them soon. She paused. 'Now that your mum is making real progress we'll soon be able to disclose the truth and get back to normal.'

He nodded contemplatively. 'But even if we get through that, and she is allowed to leave hospital in a week's time, I still have a problem. She can't stay here, in this house, on her own, and she can't go back to The Vicarage either, not yet. I have to go to London.

I've put off meetings twice already and people are starting to get cheesed off.'

'I'd stay on longer if I could, but I can't. I have to get back to work.'

'Don't give it another thought. It's my problem, not yours! I was planning to go home to check on the start of the repairs after I'd been to London, because I wanted the house to be more comfortable when she returned. Maria would call every day and help out with shopping, etc., but she'd still be alone most of the time.'

Lucy was silent, searching for a solution. 'What about a health resort of some kind? I'm sure, if you explain the situation like you did to me, she'll understand. If she agrees to the idea, ask the doctors if they can recommend somewhere for her to stay, not too far from here.'

'D'you know that's not a bad idea.' He swirled the wine around in the glass again and gauzy fragments of colour glowed like rubies in the light of the candles.

'I bet your mother wishes your dad was around at a time like this.'

In an ironic tone, he said, 'He wasn't my father.'

Lucy thought she'd misheard him; she faltered. 'What . . . what did you say?'

'He wasn't my dad.' His face was hard, the lines grew suddenly sharper.

Lucy was shocked, she didn't know what to say.

Some of the rigidity went out of his pose. As if it was an afterthought, he added. 'My mother doesn't realise I know, so please don't ever mention it to her.'

'What makes you so certain he wasn't your . . . ?'

Ethan cut in before she finished the sentence. 'I don't know the exact whys and wherefores. I've never asked Mum for details and she's never volunteered any.'

'How do you know then?'

There was a pregnant pause and he leaned forward, his hands resting on his thighs. 'I had a blazing row with my father one day. He was annoyed because I kept coming home late. I knew it was wrong of me, and that my mother worried because I did, but typical teenager, I tested my strength and stood my ground. We shouted at each other, and then his anger got the better of him, and he told me what he probably didn't intend to. He told me if he'd been my real father he would have forced me to behave differently. When the information hit my brain, I was so shocked it nailed me to the spot for a few seconds then I just left him and locked myself in a room until I'd digested it.' He turned away, to stare into the flames of the fire.

She couldn't see his face. Disconcerted and feeling slightly lost and astonished, she crossed her arms and said, 'That must have been a terrible shock. How old were you?'

'Not much fun. About sixteen!' He paused again for a fraction of a second before he continued. 'I'd often wondered before when why he seemed so distant, sometimes almost hostile, towards me. After his outburst I was able to understand things a lot better. He should never have reacted like that, of course, but I guess he couldn't jump over his own shadow.'

The feeling of unreality began to fade. 'If you're not his son . . . are you adopted, or . . . ?'

He shrugged. 'My surname is Mason, so I'm legally his son, but — oh, what the hell, it doesn't really matter. I decided my aim should be university and left as soon as I could. I decided I had to take my life into my own hands and best avoid any more confrontation or unpleasantness with him, for Mum's sake.'

'Why didn't you ask her for the truth? Surely she noticed you two didn't get on?'

'Of course she did, but a lot of children go through difficult phases at some stage or other. She probably put it down to something like that. I don't think he honestly intended to let it slip like he did, but the damage was done.'

'So, that's why you only came home on flying visits most of the time? They must have been fraught with friction too, I expect? He must have known you avoided home because of him and felt very uncomfortable with that kind of situation.'

He nodded mutely. 'I kept my visits home to a polite minimum; most of the time I never stayed more than a few hours or just overnight. As long as I knew she was fine, I accepted the consequences of keeping a healthy distance to him and the village.

'Looking back now I know he wasn't a bad character. Even though I'm not his son, he still gave me a good home, security, financed me through university and probably did the best he could generally.'

'It must have been awful.' She touched one of his hands.

He jumped, and a few drops of wine spilled over her fingers. 'It's water under the bridge now; not that important. Past actions can't be changed.'

Still disconcerted, she said. 'But don't you want to know all about your roots? Who you are.'

He shifted in his seat, shook his head and avoided her eyes. 'No, not particularly! Forget it! I've never told anyone before; I don't know why I told you. Keep it to yourself.'

'Of course I will, but I think you should ask your mother for the truth.'

'Why? I've no intention of waking sleeping dogs at this time of her life. She has some reason for not talking about it; I'm going to leave it at that.'

He picked up the wine bottle. 'Let's top up. Mum said we should be celebrating and we will. Here's to her recovery.'

She lifted her glass in his direction, but the pleasure had gone out of the evening. He started talking about other things and she followed his lead.

His disclosures bothered her; made her think back through the years. Now she understood why he left so abruptly, and why he'd avoided home visits.

During the drive to the hospital next morning Ethan told her about a forthcoming church festival in a neighbouring village, asked her to remind him to get petrol on the way back, and stopped at a roadside stand to buy his mother a bunch of bright yellow flowers. Ethan placed his arm casually around Lucy as they entered the room. Her body tingled at his touch; his hand felt warm through her dress.

Mrs Mason looked up and smiled at them. 'What lovely flowers, you spoil me.'

'Rubbish!' He gave her an affectionate peck on her cheek. 'Feeling better?'

'Much! You wouldn't believe how I enjoyed breakfast this morning.'

Eyebrows fractionally raised he said, 'That's good.'

She replied buoyantly, 'Yes, it is. I can get up for a while after lunch: Isn't it wonderful how quickly the body recovers with the right medicine?'

Ethan exchanged a smile with Lucy. 'Yes. Thank heavens!'

Mrs Mason smiled and raised herself up on an elbow. 'What are you two going to do today, apart from visiting me at the moment?'

Ethan was pleased at her progress. 'We haven't thought about it yet.'

'Go somewhere nice with Lucy, Ethan! She's supposed to be on holiday.' She paused. 'Have you two thought about the future yet? Will you live here permanently?'

Ethan didn't hesitate. His answer sounded perfectly normal. 'We don't know yet. It's an ideal place for me to write undisturbed. I wouldn't sell it; it means too much to me.'

Lucy smothered the picture of them sharing domestic bliss. This playmaking was crazy; they shouldn't have started it. She sensed that Ethan was watching her; she avoided his face and focussed on Mrs Mason. 'I'll see if I can find a vase for the flowers.'

On the road to Gerona a few days later she leaned back in contentment and stretched her arms above her head.

'Thanks, Ethan.'

An indulgent glint appeared in his eye. 'What for, brat?'

She'd given up trying to stop him sometimes talking to her as if she was still twelve years old. 'I've seen some of the real Spain; not just the tourist blah-blah!'

'That's what I intended.'

Lucy was trying hard to curb re-emerging feelings of infatuation, but it wasn't easy. 'You love it here, don't you?'

He looked across briefly. 'Yes.'

She leaned back in the seat, brushed the occasional strand of windblown hair from her face and soaked up the sunlight. 'I can understand why; the countryside hereabouts is lovely, and everyone is so friendly.'

He nodded in agreement. 'You must come and see it in spring, or in early summer.'

The idea was tempting, but Lucy knew it wouldn't be a good idea.

After breakfast next morning, she

decided to visit the long white building up on top of the hill opposite. Ethan had told her it was a monastery and the monks had even made popular CDs of Gregorian chants. He was working at the table with papers spread untidily around his laptop.

'It's a long way.' He paused. 'But I suppose it's better than you being bored.'

'Who's bored? I'm enjoying myself but I need some exercise!' She set off at a brisk pace. The morning air was fresh, and walking between the trellises was easier than she expected.

Ethan knew she'd be annoyed if she knew he was keeping an eye on her progress, but he left his work from time to time to see where she was. He refused to analyse why. The yellow blob on her jacket moved gradually uphill to the crest and a short time later he was somehow glad to note she was on her way back.

Almost home again, Lucy passed a slender young woman with waist-length black hair walking through the vines towards Antonio. Lucy smiled at her and said, 'Buena tarde!' The other girl looked back shyly and smiled, before she replied. Looking at her watch as she climbed the steps Lucy was surprised to see it was almost midday.

Ethan, pretending to be engrossed in his work, shuffled some papers and looked up from the table, when she came in. 'Well, was it worth it?'

'Umm! There's a wonderful view of the valley and of this house from up there.'

'Did you go inside?'

'No. It's only open to the public on Tuesdays.'

He grinned. 'It's more likely that they spotted you coming, put that notice up fast, then barred the doors, and locked themselves in their cells.'

Lucy swept past him with a toss of her head. 'I'm going to have a shower.'

'Need any help?'

She ignored that too. 'There's a dark-haired beauty walking through your fields.'

'A dark-haired . . . Oh, that's probably Elena, Antonio's daughter.'

After the shower, she made them coffee. 'How's the book coming along?'

Her face was pink, and a cloud of flowery perfume drifted along with the movement of her full skirt. A wide belt around her waist defined its smallness. Ethan tried to concentrate on her question. 'Actually . . . I've thought of a brilliant new turn to the plot, but I'll have to partially rewrite a couple of chapters.'

'Strike when the iron's hot! I'll visit your mother and do the shopping. I'll tell her you'll be coming in later. Get the ideas down before inspiration fades!'

He studied her face. 'Would you mind?'

Her lashes swept across her cheekbones. 'Would I suggest it if I did?'

The blue eyes held her gaze. Her thoughts spun and she moved away to look out of the window. 'When did you say your mother is going to this rehabilitation clinic?'

'End of the week. One of the doctors

there is half-English, so I think that'll help.'

'I'd like to see where she is, and know she's all right before we leave for home.'

He nodded. 'Of course, we'll go there together and I'll come back to Spain as soon as I can. Maria and Antonio will visit her, and even if their English isn't good, it'll give her a feeling she's not alone. She'll be able to travel home after Christmas. The most important improvements at The Vicarage should be finished by then.'

'She won't admit it, but I bet she'll count the days until you come back. When are we going to tell her that our engagement is a swindle?' She avoided his eyes.

'I don't know. What do you think? Tell her now? Phone her from the UK? Do it just before we leave?'

Looking resolved she said, 'Phoning is cowardly — we have to tell her face to face.'

Sometimes, like now, he felt confused

because she was taking decisions out of his hands and he didn't seem to mind. 'Yes, you're right! What do we tell her? It was all a terrible mistake, or that we found out we're not compatible?'

Lucy shook her head. 'The truth; that she misunderstood, and we kept our mouths shut not to upset her.'

He imagined his mother's reaction. 'She'll tear me apart, limb by limb!'

Lucy laughed. 'You don't have to tell her on your own, I'll be there. In a way, I started it. I just hope she won't be too angry with us.'

'She'll be livid with me, but she likes you too much to be angry with you for long.'

There wasn't much traffic on the road. The couple of days driving back and forth to the hospital, and some outings she'd undertaken locally when Ethan was busy writing, had polished her driving skills again. Parking the car in the tree-lined avenue opposite the hospital entrance, she went to the supermarket, bought some fruit and then went to the hospital.

'Hello, Lucy! On your own?'

Ethan's coming later. He's busy with his book.'

Mrs Mason laughed. 'How did you get here?'

Lucy jangled the car keys and smiled broadly. 'I feel very confident now, even if everyone is driving on the wrong side of the road!! I've brought you some fruit.'

'Lovely! I'm being spoiled.'

Mrs Mason took some knitting she'd brought from home out of the bedside cupboard. Lucy gestured at it. 'How's the knitting coming along?'

'Good! A light sweater for Ethan, for Christmas! The back is finished and I'm halfway up the front. After you've gone, I'll have lots of time to finish it off, without worrying that Ethan will burst through the door any moment. Even in Spain the evenings can be chilly.'

Lucy nodded. 'I bet it'll look terrific.'

Mrs Mason twisted the yarn around her finger, and looked up quickly at Lucy.

'Ethan says he intends coming back here as soon as he's seen his publishers, but I don't want to drag him away from you. I won't mind if he stays in the UK for Christmas, honestly.'

'Wild horses won't keep him away; he won't be gone for longer than is absolutely necessary. He wants your house to be warm and comfortable when you come back to Bramberly. He'll definitely come back here for Christmas.

'Then you must come too. You shouldn't be apart on your first Christmas together.'

Perhaps this was the right moment? Lucy was tempted to tell her the truth — that they weren't really engaged. Lucy hesitated. Ethan ought to be with her. She substituted with, 'Do you mind . . . about going to this recuperation place? Does it worry you?'

'No, not really. I'd rather go home, but the doctor has convinced me I shouldn't travel until I'm completely fit. I know Ethan will only worry if I stay alone in his house — so if he's happy, I'm happy to go. It looks more like a hotel than a clinic from the brochure!'

Lucy patted her hand. 'You always make the best of things, don't you?'

'You have to, no matter what happens.' Susan Mason stirred uneasily in the chair. 'I'm glad to talk to you on your own, Lucy. I want to be sure you know that Ethan is a complex character. Take your time to get to know him properly and be sure.'

Lucy was surprised, but answered spontaneously. 'He was always a private sort of person, and the independent life he's led has made him even more self-sufficient but we get on very, very well together.'

She smiled indulgently at Lucy's reaction. 'I'm sure Ethan wouldn't deliberately hurt you, but I'm not sure he realises just how his lifestyle will change when he gets married; I'm afraid he might be too demanding, or too impatient. I don't want you to be unhappy.'

'Don't worry. I'm quite confident about the future.'

Mrs Mason smoothed back her hair with her hand. 'I've been meaning to have a serious talk with Ethan for a couple of years — about something very important.' Lucy wondered if it was about what Ethan had already discovered, but didn't comment. 'I've decided to postpone it till after Christmas so that you can completely enjoy the first days of your engagement. He's got enough on his mind at present. It's waited this long, it can wait a couple more weeks.'

Lucy was intrigued. She flicked an imaginary speck of dirt from her skirt. 'Whatever it is — Ethan loves you, so you shouldn't worry about it too much.'

On her way home, she thought about Susan Mason and decided that she was making real progress. She called back at the supermarket to do the shopping. When she got back to the house, Ethan was still busy typing.

5

It was still early so she went to read a book in a wind-sheltered corner of the terrace. Sometime later he threw her a generous smile as he passed her on the way to the hospital. 'Need anything from town?'

She rewarded him with a smile of her own. 'No! Did you murder anyone in your book?'

He burst out laughing. 'No, but I'm thinking about it. I haven't figured how to make it a logical move, carry out the murder, and not leave too many clues in the process.'

By the time he got back she'd already prepared their evening meal.

To his surprise, Ethan found it was very pleasant to have her around. He mused that the two of them still got on extremely well. He could be himself, say what he thought, and he'd laughed more often with her than with any woman he'd known for years, even though they shared a purely platonic relationship.

He eyed Lucy. Her cheeks flushed from cooking, her hair falling gently over her cheeks. She was one of today's independent, modern women, but by instinct he knew she'd expect loyalty and commitment. She wasn't the kind to look kindly on casual affairs.

'I could get used to this. I almost understand why men get married.'

She feigned dismay. 'You'd consider getting married just for a hot meal? Surely it's more in your line to employ a full-time house-keeper, and seek other pleasures elsewhere!'

He tilted his head to the side, his eyebrows lifted. 'Hey! That's not a bad idea! All comforts and no responsibilities.'

'You're not good husband material Ethan; in fact you'd be a disaster. Living with you would make too many demands on any woman. It's just as well that you're remaining single.'

He laughed. 'Unless I get the right offer, from the right woman . . . want to put in a bid?'

She coloured fiercely. 'Me? I'm not crazy.'

The day before their flight home, they drove together to see Mrs Mason's new habitat, and saw a worried looking Mrs Mason. Lucy was puzzled. The room looked comfortable; it was furnished in shades of pale green and pink and a small terrace looked out across fields to a nearby wood. She even had her own TV with satellite reception.

'Hello! Is something the matter? You look upset.'

The older woman's face was pale. 'I've done something awful! I've jumped the gun.'

Puzzled and trying to calm her, Lucy said, 'What do you mean exactly?'

'I'm afraid I've put my foot in it.' Ethan and Lucy waited patiently. 'I phoned Lucy's mother last night to say how pleased I was.'

Lucy drew a deep breath, her fingernails bit into her palms. Ethan paused before he said, 'And they were surprised to hear about our engagement?'

'Yes, shocked! I'm sorry. I assumed everyone knew. I thought it was too late to ring you last night, but I couldn't sleep afterwards.'

Ethan said with deceptive calm, 'It's nothing for you to get so upset about, is it, Lucy?' He eyed her beseechingly.

Recovering, she looked at them both and shook her head automatically.

'Why didn't they know? Why haven't you told them?'

Ethan's writing abilities seemed to stand him in good stead. 'We kept putting it off, and in the end we decided it would be nicer to tell them face-to-face.'

Lucy added, 'We were planning to tell them tomorrow.'

'I must say, if they're angry, I'm on their side. You should have told them before now.'

Lucy cleared her throat. 'H . . . how did my mother react?'

'It took her breath away; there was dead silence, and I thought we'd been disconnected. Then she asked if she'd understood properly. She soon perked up though. We tried to guess why you hadn't told them, but in the end she said the main thing was you were happy.'

Ethan came to stand behind Lucy and put an arm around her. He squeezed her shoulder briefly. Lucy searched for a straw to clutch at; something to divert her mind from the disorder. 'This is a lovely room! The view from the balcony is beautiful.'

'Yes, it is, isn't it?' She looked at Lucy. 'You're not too mad with me, for phoning your parents?'

Lucy put some sincerity into her voice. 'No . . . no of course not! Time went so fast and we kept putting it off because we were busy with all sorts of other things. In the end we decided it'd be nicer to tell them face-to-face. I'm certain that they'll be pleased; they've always liked Ethan very much, and they know him so well.'

Later when they returned to the car for the journey home, Ethan sank into the seat and closed the car door. He didn't start the engine.

Lucy broke the silence. 'It's appalling! If my parents know, the rest of the village does too.'

He stared ahead into the darkness and said quietly, 'To be honest your family is my only worry! How will they react if we say it was just a well-meant deception?'

She swallowed hard. 'Are you kidding? My parents will skin me alive!'

He was silent for a moment, his hands on the wheel. 'Then we carry on.'

'What! Are you completely mad?'

With quiet but desperate firmness, he said. 'It's the only way out. They think we're engaged — so we're engaged!'

'Carry on? What on earth are you talking about?'

'We'll continue, and break it off later on; say it was a mistake.'

Clenching her teeth, she said. 'It's already one hell of a mistake. We'll only make things worse.'

He snapped. 'Your mother has broadcast the news to everyone in that village by now. If she is forced to tell them we're not engaged after all, she'll look stupid. I won't let that happen.'

She answered in a rush of words. 'We must face the music eventually, why not now?'

'No one will understand, that's why. Admitting to people that we deliberately lied, and didn't clear it with my mother at the earliest opportunity will be more difficult than continuing the charade, and squabbling our way out of it in a couple of months' time.'

Her fingers locked tightly in her lap. 'We wait, and when the dust has settled, we tell them it was all a lie? I don't get it? What's the difference between telling them now or later?'

'They'll not know it was a lie, that's

the difference! When we break off the engagement, they'll believe it was a genuine one. Breaking off a seemingly genuine engagement will cause less heartache for everyone than admitting that it was a downright lie from the start.'

They sat in silence. Lucy looked at someone hurrying past the car. 'I'm so sorry, Ethan. What a mess! I feel so responsible. I only wanted to help your mother at a critical moment, and it's all gone out of control.'

His voice was encouraging. 'Hey! It's my fault as much as yours and it's not the end of the world.'

She took a deep breath. 'Huh! And how am I supposed to convince my mother we're in love?'

He laughed. 'Use your imagination, or read up on how you're supposed to feel, you're a librarian.'

The flight home was uneventful. Lucy's trepidation increased with every passing mile and by the time they were actually in front of her parents' house she was dreading everyone's reaction. She threw back her shoulders and mounted the steps. She didn't need her key; the door flew open. Lucy coloured as she met her mother's eyes and she was lost for words; she knew it would be difficult. Ethan stepped in front of her and kissed Mrs Waring's cheek.

'Don't be angry. We're sorry you heard about it from my mother like that, but our only excuse is we thought we wanted to tell you face to face and not over the phone.'

Lucy's mother looked up at him and couldn't resist. Lucy could only guess he was smiling, she couldn't see his face. Mrs Waring's eyes twinkled. 'True, I was miffed, but there isn't any man I'd welcome more into this family than you, Ethan.' She gave him a hug.

Lucy's father hovered in the background; he pulled Ethan forward and took his hand. 'Come in, lad! You've always been welcome here, and I couldn't wish for a better son-in-law. It's great news! Where's my Lucy?'

Lucy was in her mother's arms with misted eyes, and then she walked to her father's bear-like hug and hid her face against his chest. She heard Colin's voice in the sitting room and pulled herself free to follow Ethan. It was all so much harder than she'd imagined. Colin was beaming, thumping Ethan on the back and when he saw her, he picked her up.

'Talk about clandestine behaviour . . .'

Lucy's cheeks grew pink. She caught Ethan's eye.

Ethan continued to take the brunt of it, and took the edge off any tension. 'It took my breath away too. I didn't stand a chance! She had me walking the plank before I realised it.'

Colin nodded knowingly. He grinned. 'Don't tell me, I know all about it.'

Judy came forward with Tim in her arms to kiss Lucy and Ethan. Glasses were passed around. Her father's voice drifted across the room. 'Here's to Lucy and Ethan!'

Lucy had a lump in her throat. She

felt such a miserable cheat and hated deceiving them.

'How's your mother, Ethan?' Mrs Waring motioned them towards the sofa, and Ethan sat down next to Lucy, draping one arm casually around her shoulders.

'Much better thanks; making real progress now.'

'It was sensible to let her stay and convalesce, but I'm sure she wishes she was here today. Give me her number. I'll ring her later and tell her about it and that you arrived safely.'

'No ring Lucy?' Judy broke in.

Lucy was taken aback, she hadn't thought about a ring. Ethan reacted quickly. 'I didn't plan to ask Lucy to marry me, and I certainly didn't have a ring in my pocket when I did. We'll sort that out together.' He pulled her closer; acting his part to perfection.

Lucy's mother was an excellent cook, and had made an extra effort. The traditional meal of roasted lamb flavoured with rosemary, with golden potatoes, Brussels sprouts, mushrooms and carrots, was perfect. They sat at the table after talking about Mrs Mason's illness, and catching up on local happenings.

Eventually, Colin and Judy left when it was time to put Tim to bed. It was late before Ethan rose. Lucy went with him to the door.

One hand on the door knob, he said, 'See you tomorrow? You start work again on Monday, don't you?'

'Yes.' Awkwardly, she looked at him. 'I don't want to get in your way.'

Ethan was beginning to think she could never get in the way, but that was a dangerous line of thought. He traced the side of her face and the dusty rose of her cheeks with his finger instead. 'We're engaged; it would seem odd if we didn't want to see one another all the time.'

She wanted to shy away from his nearness; her stomach churned. 'OK, see you!'

He bent his head and lifted her face

with a crooked finger. 'Just in case someone's watching!' He gave her a fleeting kiss and realised it wasn't an irksome task.

Lucy's stomach did another somersault. He lifted his head and looked at her, before he kissed her briefly on her forehead and disappeared.

★   ★   ★

'Congratulations! What good news! I've a small present for you, my dear.'

She accepted the parcel and opened it to find a pair of powder-blue towels. 'Mrs Lewis, how kind! Thank you very much.'

The woman brushed her thanks aside. 'My pleasure; when you get married you'll get a matching bath towel. You can never have enough towels. Well I'll be off, got to make my hubby's tea. Your fiancé is a handsome fellow. I hope he knows how lucky he is.'

Regular library users had surprised Lucy. So far she'd received teacloths, a rolling pin, a cookery book, and a salad bowl. She showed Ethan the latest addition on her way home.

'I feel so guilty. I label them and put them in the drawer — ready to give them back.'

He shrugged. 'Not much else you can do, is there?' They were in the living room. The table, carpet and various other surfaces were plastered with photos and papers.

Lucy looked round intriguingly. 'What's going on?'

He was reluctant to explain but he did. 'I was looking for clues about my origins.'

Her heart went out to him. 'Ethan! Why don't you just ask your mother?'

He shook his head, and started to bundle the papers and stack the photo-albums. 'I'm curious, but it's not so important. I thought there would be something obvious. Forget it!'

She guessed he wanted to avoid more questions. 'Did you find anything of interest?'

'Not much. There are so many photos of people and places I don't recognise. My mother came from Cornwall. I bet you don't know all the people in your family albums either. That's how it is.' He paused. 'How about going to the pictures?' He was changing the theme.

'If you like.' She tilted her head and felt she'd never known any man better.

With his hands in his pockets, he asked, 'Ah . . . talking about the cinema! I meant to ask — what about . . . what was his name? How did he react? Does he know about our engagement?'

'Lance? I phoned and said I wouldn't be seeing him again, for obvious reasons. He told me he'd heard about our engagement, and congratulated me rather stiffly. I felt awful.'

'Didn't he protest? He must be feeble to let you go like that, without a fight.'

'He didn't deserve to be treated badly. He wasn't cowardly; he was a gentleman.'

'Hmm! I hope you didn't like him too much? It might be hard to reverse things later.'

She looked nonchalant. 'No. I liked him, but I don't feel grief-stricken that I won't be his girlfriend anymore.' Ethan realised he was relieved.

It was an action-film full of gunfights, exploding bombs and supermen; Ethan enjoyed it immensely. Afterwards they called at the local pub on the way home.

'Hello!' Rachael's voice startled them both.

Ethan looked up. 'Hi Rachael. What are you doing here?'

'I'm with some friends over there.' She indicated a group of people sitting around the blazing fire. Without invitation, she draped herself elegantly in a chair next to Ethan. 'I hear congratulations are in order. I wondered why I hadn't heard from you about the contract.' She looked briefly at Lucy and smiled. 'I was surprised. You gave me the impression you were childhood friends, nothing more, and I thought you weren't the marrying kind, Ethan?'

Ethan looked unperturbed and gave her a lopsided smile. When he smiled at Lucy like that her legs turned to jelly. 'We're all surprised by what life has in store for us, aren't we?'

Rachael smiled uncertainly, and got up. Speaking to Ethan, she said, 'The contract is waiting for you to sign. I'll put in the post tomorrow.'

Lucy followed her with her eyes as she moved back to her friends.

Ethan was amused by the expression on Lucy's face and he began to chuckle. 'You don't like her, do you? Why not?'

Awkwardly she cleared her throat. 'I only met her once at your house. Why should I dislike her?'

He shrugged. 'I suspect it's just a female thing! Perhaps you're worried that she'll lead me astray?'

'Please, don't bother because of me. In fact it would provide us with an ideal reason to break up!'

He laughed and kissed her quickly on the tip of her nose, leaning across the table.

'You go pink when you're angry! Let's go home.'

She heard the laughter in his voice and tried to be unconcerned as he helped her on with her coat. He couldn't have been so jovial if he knew how her interest in him was growing. Towards the end of the week, he went up to London to see his agent and then on to Spain for a long weekend to see his mother. He was away for a week and Lucy missed him a lot.

6

She went to meet him at the station when he returned, and it wasn't at all difficult to act the happy fiancée. Her heart beat furiously when she spotted him getting off the train. She must pull herself together — one day this game would end and she knew already she'd be left with a lot of problems. At the moment it was easy to forget and just play along.

In the days that followed, Lucy continued to enjoy his company, and ignored the voices inside that sent her warning signals all the time. One day, on her way home from work, she spotted Rachael's car parked in the drive. He'd mentioned one of the paragraphs in his latest contract needed correction, but Lucy felt irritated to know they were on their own. Why couldn't Ethan go to Rachael's office, like the other clients?

* ★ ★ ★

'Are you coming to Spain or not? I can't wait much longer or I won't get a seat myself.'

Lucy wavered. 'My parents expect me to, but it's such a sham. I feel so guilty.'

He studied her for a moment. 'If you like, we can start to bicker and quarrel in public after Christmas. A couple of weeks of that and then they won't be in for a surprise when we break up.' Ethan found the prospect was a dismal one.

'You're sure you don't mind me coming?'

'Lucy! I've got used to you; in fact, I think it'll be strange to be single again.'

'I know what you mean.'

★ ★ ★

Lucy leaned back in the seat in the economy class and looked down at her left hand. 'It's a very unusual ring, isn't it?'

'My mother kept asking if I'd bought

a ring, and I kept putting her off with excuses that we couldn't find the right one. Then she suggested that one, and told me where to find it. A family heirloom as they say.'

'I think it's lovely.'

'I've never seen my mother wearing it. Wonder where it comes from?'

'It's a good solution though. You can give it back to her when we break up, anything else would have been a waste of money.'

They were soon in Spain and speeding towards his home. The head-lights lit up the darkness and Lucy looked forward to them being alone under the same roof again.

He picked up their suitcases and headed for the steps. It was familiar territory now; Lucy trotted confidently behind him. She took off her coat and hung it in the narrow wardrobe in her room. She followed some appetising smells coming from the kitchen, and found Ethan already laying the table.

'Maria left us something in the oven.

What a wonderful woman she is!'

'Buy her a nice Christmas present. She must be extremely busy at this time of year.'

'I will. She's one of the few women I couldn't do without.'

The meal was delicious, a beef ragout, with lots of steaming vegetables.

'When are you picking your mum up from the clinic?'

'I'll call tomorrow, see how she is, and complete the formalities. I know that she wants to stay for a special Christmas concert tomorrow evening. We're invited too, if we like. I'll bring her back here Sunday morning.'

'Go to see her on your own tomorrow; she'd like that. Don't forget we'll have to decide about menus for the next couple of days and do some shopping.'

'If we make a list tonight, I'll shop on the way back. I'll have to call in at the co-operative anyway, to check on things too.'

'Can you still afford the time to help them?'

'Not really. I'd like to hand it over, but there isn't anyone else locally who would do it as far as I know. They don't pay much but I can't let them down.'

Next morning, she slept late. By the time she got up Ethan had left. A note told her he had their list, and if there was anything missing, they'd have to get it later that afternoon.

They'd brought some typical British Christmas fare with them, but she decided that another cake would be a welcome addition. She saw there were basic ingredients like butter, flour and eggs in the kitchen so she made a chocolate sponge and left it to cool on the rack.

She cleared the kitchen, and decided to go for a walk. She went out to the terrace to check the weather, a figure was moving through the vines, coming up towards the house. At first, Lucy didn't recognise her; then she waved and called, 'Hello, Elena. What are you doing here?'

'I took eggs to my aunt, and now I

take a short-cut to the village to see my gran.'

'The path behind the house?'

The girl nodded. 'I see Ethan driving away this morning?'

'Yes.' Lucy nodded. 'He's gone to see his mother.'

'So you're alone?'

'Yes. I was going for a walk, but come in and have some coffee.'

Shyly Elena accepted and came up the steps. They sat at the kitchen table sipping from thick ceramic mugs.

'Where do you work, Elena?'

'Oh, here and there. There are not many jobs for young people around here.' Her voice brightened. 'But I go to Ampuri-abrava after Christmas to work in a hotel. One day I'd like to be a receptionist.'

'Somewhere on the Costa Brava?'

'Yes. Lots of tourists, lots of money, lots of tips.'

She didn't like to be disheartening, but Lucy was a realist. 'Lots of work, too!'

She shrugged. 'You and Ethan are,

how you say, engaged?'

'Yes.' Lucy guessed Elena had heard it from Maria, and Maria from Ethan's mother.

'He will stay in Spain. So you come here too?'

Lucy felt uncomfortable. 'We haven't made plans yet. I expect so.'

Elena nodded and looked at the clock on the wall and got up. 'I must go. I promise to help with the baking for the holiday.'

Lucy nodded and smiled. She got up and put their mugs in the sink, before she wrapped a scarf loosely round her neck and slipped into a jacket. 'I'll come some of the way with you.'

They climbed the hill together until Elena branched off towards the village and Lucy set off in the opposite direction. She tried to note where she was going for the return journey. The grass was hard and dry underfoot and thorny bushes grew between jagged protruding boulders.

There was a barely noticeable foot-worn pathway, but at least it was an indication that other people came this way. At this time of year with the wind whistling in her ears, the place seemed wild and inhospitable.

After she'd been walking for about half-an-hour she looked back. In summer this was probably an attractive spot. She sat down in the shelter of the stones. Cut off from the wind, the sun was warm on her face. She lay back on the grass and closed her eyes.

She woke; it felt like a few seconds, but she must have slept a long time because the afternoon sun was fading. She looked at her watch and was surprised to see how late it was. She started back down the track, walking briskly and looking for familiar features. From here, it was a long way down to the floor of the valley, and the terrain was all unfamiliar. Where was the fork in the path surely she should have reached it by now? Soon, she knew that she must have missed the way completely. She also knew she had to find recognisable features soon because darkness was descending much faster than she expected.

Ethan would wonder where she was when he got back, and at some stage he'd start to worry, but even if he searched, he'd never think of looking for her up here. It was far from the house and from the village.

Lucy turned towards an outcrop of a group of rocks she'd just passed; she was happy to find a kind of shallow cavity in one of them that cut off some of the wind. It wasn't much, but at least it was a little protection.

When daylight faded completely Lucy couldn't decide what was more frightening, the darkness, the isolation, or the cold. Trying not to feel frightened, the cold crept through her body. At first she just turned away from the wind and tried to wrap her coat and scarf even tighter round herself. Despite her attempts at slapping her body with her arms, and stamping her feet to keep the circulation going, gradually her body just felt like an icicle.

Sometime later the sounds of movement and of voices drifted towards her softly on the wings of the wind. She'd dozed but was too cold and scared to give in to sleep. Her throat was dry and although she wanted to call out, nothing emerged except a feeble croaking. She was still crouched awkwardly beneath the rocks, when torchlight slashed through the darkness and picked her out in her hiding place.

She was blinded her for a moment. A couple of Spanish voices shouted back to the others trampling through the undergrowth behind them. Excited voices advanced; everyone wanted to be in on the moment of discovery. She couldn't see him, but she heard Ethan's voice and had never felt more relieved. She was so glad to feel the warmth of his body.

'Lucy! Lucy! Are you all right? Say something!'

She relaxed within the circle of his arms; he felt so wonderfully solid and familiar. When she started to pull back after a few seconds, he stopped her, holding her protectively.

'Stay right where you are.'

'Hello, Ethan!' Her voice sounded hoarse.

Someone handed him something and he lifted it to her lips.

'Here drink some of this.'

She spluttered as she took a sip. The flask contained hot coffee laced with brandy. She felt instant warmth spreading from her throat to her stomach. 'H . . . how did you f . . . find me?'

'Never mind. It's not important now. Take another sip.' As she gripped the flask, he slipped off his jacket and placed it around her shoulders.

'You walked in the wrong direction. We'll go back by road; ironically it isn't far from here to the house, just over that ridge. It won't take long to get you home.'

His arm slipped around her waist and she leaned against home.

Once they'd made it to the car, the journey back to Ethan's house was fast.

Sitting with a rug wrapped around her legs, and the heating going at full blast, she leaned back and closed her eyes. She thought how glad she was to be out of the cold, and to be here with Ethan. The light in the living room blinded her for a moment until she'd adjusted.

She could see his face properly again; his skin was drawn tightly across his cheekbones, and his blue eyes were full of shadows. She smiled at him feebly. He helped her out of the jacket and shoved her towards the fireplace. He threw on some more logs and began to rub her hands. 'You're a block of ice, but that's not surprising.'

'It's so warm here; it's wonderful to be out of the cold.'

'I'm going to run you a hot bath; then you can get straight into bed before I make you something to eat. Poached egg on toast and tea?'

Her face lightened. 'That sounds fantastic.'

He touched her cheek gently with his finger before he went. Sliding beneath the water the warmth had a miraculous effect. She felt drowsy, comfortable, and cared-for.

He came into her room later, with a tray and pushed the bedside lamp aside to make room for it. She looked longingly at the poached eggs, and hot toast.

He watched until she began to eat and then left with a smile. Lucy was soon contented, warm, and fed; it was easy to fall into a deep and dreamless sleep.

She didn't often wake in the middle of the night, but her body was still reacting to the effects of the last couple of hours. Daylight was still far off. He must have heard the bathroom door opening and closing. He peeped around the bedroom door questioningly. She was staring up at the ceiling, but smiled when she noticed him.

'Feeling better?'

'Yes, much. Did I disturb you? Sorry for all the trouble I've caused.' She sat up and he settled himself on the edge of the bed.

'Want to talk about it?'

'There isn't much to tell; I got lost. How did you find me?'

'When I got back, I eventually noticed the two mugs in the sink. I wondered who'd called. I thought it might be Maria, and you'd gone with her for some reason.' He reached out and took her hand in his. 'I waited; thought you'd walk in the door any minute. When it got dark, I started to worry and went to Maria's. She hadn't seen you, but Elena told me you'd walked together, until she branched off towards the village and you went in the other direction.'

Unconsciously his thumb rubbed the back of her hand. Lucy felt her heart stirring.

'Antonio helped me organise a search party, and the rest is history.'

She shuddered. I didn't realise darkness and silence could be frightening, I was really scared.' She looked down to avoid his eyes.

He reached forward and folded her gently into his arms stroking her hair away from her forehead with his hands. 'It's understandable, but you're safe now Lucy.' He kissed her gently on her forehead and brushed her cheeks with the edge of his thumb. They suddenly knew they were powerless and his mouth covered hers.

7

The early morning sunlight bathed the room in a yellow glow and the white curtains were moving gently in the breeze. Ethan sat on the side of the bed, staring silently ahead. Love made you susceptible and weak. Too much involvement meant someone else held power over you and he intended to be in control of his own life.

But this time it was completely different; this time it was Lucy. He didn't need to think whether he liked her or not, he liked her more than any woman he'd ever met, but that didn't mean he wanted her to take over his life.

He definitely didn't intend to string her along. He'd been foolish — they'd been foolish. The relief after finding her safe last night had generated a very emotional situation in them both. He ran his fingers through his hair.

He had to make things clear to her before she expected too much of him. He was a loner; a self-centred egoist.

The air was heavy with emotion and she noticed him fighting to find the right words. A flicker of apprehension coursed through her and she felt intuitively, as her dismay grew, that the bottom was about to fall out of her world.

He ran a hand down his face and his expression was tight with strain. His voice thickened. 'I'm sorry!'

Somewhere her brain registered that he was telling her she was no one special. She was a mistake. They were friends, good friends, but he didn't love her. She shut her eyes briefly in an effort to control her disappointment.

'Perhaps I should have remembered your attitude to women and to relationships. You once said that it's pointless to look back and regret. You're right, so let's move on.'

Her voice was full of unspoken

regrets, hidden meanings. Her throat felt like sandpaper. 'Don't worry, I understand, No scenes, no reproaches. We're both responsible adults!'

His fists were clenched. 'It's not easy to explain. You're a special person Lucy, but not in a romantic way.'

'I said I understand, and I do! Stop trying to explain everything!' Her voice wavered and was beginning to shake slightly. She hoped he didn't notice; she had to end the conversation.

Perhaps he could carry on as if nothing had happened, but she couldn't. She had to make plans, and fast. She showered and dressed, bundled her pyjamas into her suitcase, and pushed his Christmas present into a corner and slammed the lid. Her thoughts moved in restless circles. He'd not once mentioned the word love, not even hinted at it.

Once her room was tidy, Lucy walked to the living room. To her relief it was empty. She flipped through the pages of the telephone book. Her ears picked up the faint sound of movement in the kitchen. She dialled a number; spoke to someone who understood enough English to connect her to a booking clerk. There were two last-minute cancellations on a flight to Gatwick. Lucy gave the woman the details of her credit card and booked one of them.

She threw back her shoulders, walked purposely to the kitchen. He was sitting at the table. Out of the corner of her eye, she noticed that he was listlessly stirring a mug of coffee in never-ending circles with a silver spoon. The air was charged and she knew things would never be the same again. 'I've booked a flight leaving at eleven. Will you take me to the airport, please?'

He looked shocked. 'Why?'

'Come on, Ethan! You know your mother will pick up the atmosphere. I'd rather go home before she comes.'

'How will you explain your sudden return?'

'I'll do what we should have done long ago, tell them we had a blazing row, and we broke the engagement.'

His voice sounded casual, even to his own ears. 'Coffee's ready. Sit down. Let's talk. Let's not part in anger.'

'No time; we've said what needs to be said. We both know where we stand. I'm not angry.' She turned, and was glad to escape. 'I have to pack, there isn't much time.'

She went towards her room again and Ethan knew she was providing a way out of the dilemma for them both. Half an hour later her suitcase was in the boot of the car, and they were travelling down the bumpy track towards the main road.

On arrival, she got out and began to rummage through her shoulder bag for her passport. Ethan lifted her luggage out of the boot and put it on the pavement in front of her. He noted that she was pale and there were faint circles under her eyes. He had a sudden urge to reach out, to touch her cheek.

'Thanks! Don't wait! I'm fine. Wish your mum a Merry Christmas; I've left her present in the living room.' She turned to go.

His lips were a thin line and his skin was stretched taut and white over his cheekbones. His shoulders tensed and he shoved his hands into his pockets.

She walked swiftly towards the departure lounge, jerking her suitcase forcefully behind her. He stared after her; other people crossed back and forth between them and interrupted his view. The glass doors shut behind her with a soft whooshing noise. She didn't look back. Inside the building, she spotted the sign for the appropriate airline and hurried toward it.

A short time later Ethan was on the outskirts of the airport, and tried to re-orientate his thoughts. Now he may as well do a detour, and pick up his mother from the nursing home on the way back, then the house wouldn't seem so empty. How would she react? Lucy circled his brain and he kept wondering why everything had gone so terribly wrong?

He realised he'd hurt her badly. One thought dismayed him more than any other; the two of them could never return to that free-and-easy, special friendship, they'd had before.

He'd lied to himself, ignored what had been growing in him for weeks. He was in love for the first time in his life — with Lucy. He breathed in quick shallow gasps, dumbstruck by his own stupidity.

On her way home, some of the bitterness and anger settled and she began to think more clearly. She had to admit she'd always known he didn't seek a serious relationship. Was he to blame if she chose to believe what she wanted to, and didn't accept the reality as it was? She had no right to expect he'd love her just because she loved him.

Glancing down at her hand, she saw she was still wearing the engagement ring. She rubbed the surface of the sapphire and diamonds absentmindedly, took it off and put it in a side pocket of her handbag. She'd give it back to Mrs Mason when she came home from Spain. Thoughts of how sad Susan Mason would be made her feel even more miserable, if that was possible.

She took a deep breath, forced her lips into a curved stiff smile as she climbed the steps to the front door. With a sinking heart, she registered the understandable surprise caused by her sudden appearance in the living room. Her father was first to speak. 'Lucy, what on earth . . . ?'

Lucy spoke with quiet but desperate firmness and explained they'd quarrelled and that the engagement was over. Her father looked helpless and her mother was dumbstruck for a moment, but then enfolded her in her arms. 'Oh, Lucy! All couples go through rough patches now and then, things will look different in a couple of day's time.'

'No, Mum, we're just not suited. We want different things from life.' Lucy gave way to pent-up feelings at last and burst into tears.

Christmas was terrible, even if Tim managed to disperse some misery with the joy in his face as he opened his presents after Christmas lunch. The family's support was her lifeline to reality. Other things in life were more important than Ethan; she'd find what and where, then she could start to live a normal life again.

After Christmas she was ill with flu; no doubt this was the result of her night out on the hillside in Spain. When she returned to work, things followed a normal routine again. She knew her best friend, Pam, was waiting to hear the details and offer sympathy and consolation, but the truth was hers and Ethan's, and it would stay that way.

Lucy got a letter from Ethan's mum.

I'm sure you know that I'm terribly sorry that you and Ethan decided to break your engagement. Needless to say I wish it wasn't true, but I hope that we'll continue to be friends and that you'll come and visit me when I'm home again.

I'd be very upset if I thought we were driven apart by something that neither you, nor I, could anticipate. — Love Susan Mason.

Everything was reorganised and up to date at the library. Lucy had time on her hands to catch up on articles in professional magazines. One day an advertisement for qualified librarians to catalogue a private library of books caught her eye. That's what she needed, a new perspective, a new beginning. She applied to the box number and waited.

8

A week later a letter arrived inviting her to an interview. Waiting in the lobby of the hotel, Lucy hoped that her dark blue tailored trouser suit and soft white blouse made the right sort of impression. A middle-aged, white-haired man in a conservative suit and public school tie came to fetch her.

'Good morning, my name is Henry Walters. You are Lucy Waring?' Lucy nodded. 'This way please.' She followed him into a nearby conference room. 'Please sit down, and make yourself comfortable.' Lucy did. 'Your qualifications and references are good. You realise this is a job for six months? There's no guarantee we can offer you anything else afterwards.'

Lucy nodded. 'I know. I'm still interested.'

'You have to classify and list the

contents of the library ready for auction. If they're pre-sorted into categories and authors, we'll try to sell them 'bundled' rather than trying to sell individual books. We're hoping interested booksellers might buy most of them before we go to auction. First editions or rare copies will be auctioned, of course. It must be done as quickly as possible and without constant supervision.'

'I'll do my very best.'

'I've asked people how much time you need — people who've worked on similar jobs before, and I've added some leeway for unforeseen problems. The catalogues have to be ready for the printers several weeks before the actual auction date in early August. Our seller will try to get rid of most of these books beforehand. He'll keep in touch and you can give him listings of what you've sorted from time to time. If he sells some, you'll need to adjust your lists accordingly.'

Lucy smiled at him. 'It sounds like a challenge.'

'Accommodation and meals on the job are part of the salary, but if you prefer you can live elsewhere, we'll adjust the salary accordingly.'

'That sounds fair.'

'You're still interested? When's the earliest date you could start?'

'Yes . . . yes I am. I've already checked; in four weeks time.'

Mr Walters checked his pocket calculator. 'That would suit us very well. Will you give me a definite date, and let me know?'

'Yes, of course.'

'Any questions?'

'Am I on my own?'

'Oh, I'm sorry, I should have mentioned that. No, there'll be someone else, and the two of you will have to organise everything between you.' He paused. 'I think you'll be highly suitable. I'd like to offer you the job.'

Lucy was delighted. 'And I'll be pleased to accept.'

He nodded. He took out his wallet. 'Good. Here's my card. Let me know exact dates and then I'll send you a contract and the rest of the information.'

On the way home, she felt pleased that her life was going in a new direction. She was totally miserable about what had happened between her and Ethan, but now she had something new to think about. Why hadn't she done something like this before?

Her parents were surprised that she'd accepted the job outright, but guessed her motives. Lucy decided to buy her own car. She'd often thought about it, but up to now it had seemed a waste of money. Glancing up the drive when she passed, she saw that Mrs Mason's house was still deserted, and it was dark there at night, but during the day the firms were busy. She was glad to be going away.

Following the directions she found the mansion at the end of a winding narrow country lane bordered by hawthorn hedges harbouring the first sprinkling of green buds. The house was a beautiful Georgian building in the middle of some magnificent old parkland.

The housekeeper showed Lucy to her room. It was comfortable and warm. Lucy unpacked her suitcase and looked forward to meeting her new colleague. The evening meal was served at six-thirty in a small room on the ground floor. When she entered it was empty, and she studied the oriental carpet in shades of red and blue, the wooden panelling and the sumptuous velvet curtains framing the long windows. A few minutes later, a young woman came in. 'Hello, I'm Margaret, Margaret Ashton. You must be my fellow worker?'

Lucy smiled. 'Yes. I'm Lucy Waring.'

Her companion looked around. 'Quite an impressive place, isn't it?'

'Yes, if the furniture is anything to go by.'

They exchanged details about themselves. Lucy thought Margaret was open and friendly, and she showed a spirited disposition that matched her curly red hair.

'It's a bit off the beaten track here,

isn't it? But I presume there's a local pub so we ought to be able to get away from the ghosts and ghouls now and then, but we'll need a really good torch to find the way down the drive to the village in the dark.'

'I have a car.'

'Really? Super! We'll be able to go to the cinema then, or into Bath. It's not that far ... Oh, sorry! I'm being presumptuous, aren't I?'

Lucy laughed. 'Not at all; it's a good idea.'

The housekeeper pushed a serving trolley into the room, and they found the food was good and plentiful. Margaret continued to chatter and Lucy was determined to enjoy this new phase of her life.

The library was huge, and in the course of time, seemed to have been abandoned. First of all they worked out roughly how much time they had, to re-sort and list. Thanks to a computer, they were able to start right away. By the end of the first week they'd finished one floor to ceiling section and found some interesting first editions. Feeding details into the computer took time and all their concentration.

Lucy went home the first weekend — it was bliss to sleep late and be pampered by the extra attention she got. Lucy's mother told her that Ethan's mother had returned; she'd met her down the village. Lucy decided it was time to close the gap, and return the ring. She didn't ask her mother what she really wanted to know — if Ethan had come back too. A strange car was in front of the door when she walked up the drive.

Her heart pounded uncontrollably, she had the urge to turn around and run away, but she didn't. The house now had new windows and a new door and looked a lot smarter. When Mrs Mason answered the doorbell she opened her arms, and Lucy walked into them to be hugged tightly. Lucy's eyes glistened.

'Oh, I'm so glad Lucy. I was afraid

you wouldn't come again.'

'I want to. I've been coming here so long. It's part of my life. I can't stop.'

'Come in!' Mrs Mason bustled off to the kitchen and Lucy hung her coat on the hallstand. She went into the living-room and sat down.

A few minutes later Susan Mason joined her. 'It's lovely and warm here now. What a difference properly fitting doors and windows make. Ethan's had a new central heating system installed too; much simpler to use than the old one. I'm afraid Mrs Evans had to do a lot of extra cleaning but I feel very comfortable now.'

'Are you really better now? Fully recovered from your illness?'

'Yes, of course. I feel very fit. Ethan tried to persuade me to stay in Spain until the spring, but I wanted to come home. I've been away too long.'

'You're a homebird, and I'm sure you missed the village.'

'Yes, I was sorry to hear that you'd left.' She paused. 'But after what happened I understand. Your mother tells me that you have a new job near Bath. How exciting. I'm looking forward to hearing all about it.'

Lucy searched in her pocket and handed Mrs Mason the ring. 'First . . . before I forget, your ring! I should have given it to Ethan, but in the confusion before I left . . . I decided to bring it back to you personally, because he told me it was yours anyway.'

Mrs Mason took the ring and held it gingerly between the thumb and finger of one hand. 'I wish I'd never suggested this ring to Ethan now. It brings bad luck.'

Lucy was puzzled. 'Bad luck, what do you mean back luck?'

'This was my engagement ring. I got it from Ethan's father.'

'From Mr Mason?'

'No, I was engaged to someone else, before I married Thomas. He died before we could get married.'

'Oh, how awful! What happened?'

'He was such a special man; caring,

thoughtful, loving and quite wonderful. He was a member of a lifeboat crew. He went out on a rescue mission one stormy night and was swept overboard. His body was never found.'

Lucy's voice echoed her surprise and shock. 'How dreadful!'

'Yes, even after a lifetime, the memories are still vivid. I wanted to die at the time, until I realised I was pregnant with his child. Then I had something to live for again.'

Lucy waited, putting two and two together and asked quietly. 'He was Ethan's father?'

Susan Mason nodded.

'But you married Mr Mason. When . . . did that happen?'

'Thomas? I'd met Thomas some time before that; he'd come on holiday to our village a couple of times. I wasn't in love with him, but I liked him and he became a friend, a very good friend. When I was pregnant I had to talk to someone; so I wrote him a letter and poured out all my worries and cares. I thought he'd be able to give me some advice on how to cope on my own.

'In those days an illegitimate child was a stigma, and I realised I'd have to leave the village, so that my parents wouldn't be penalised. Nowadays no-one would bat an eyelid. I decided I either had to fight through on my own some-how, or give my baby up for adoption. I was determined to keep it, no matter what I had to do.'

Lucy nodded. 'And what happened then?'

'To my astonishment, Thomas offered to marry me and accept the child as his own. I took the easy way out and married Thomas. Later I realised just how generous a gesture it was. Not many men would have done the same. I never loved Thomas in the way I'd loved Ethan's father. I liked him very much and respected him, but love is something completely different. We still managed to have a good marriage because I think he genuinely loved me, and I liked him enough to want our marriage to be a success.'

Lucy could tell she was extremely nervous. Her fingers were still twisting the ring around and she stared at it continuously. There were spots of bright colour on her cheeks, and her voice sounded fast and excited. 'Thomas appeared to be a cold, distant man to most people but he was always kind to me, Lucy; thoughtful and considerate. I did my best to be a good wife, but I never forgot Ethan and I insisted on naming the baby after him. Thomas and I never had any children of our own so perhaps in hindsight that wasn't a very diplomatic decision either, but at the time it was the only gift I could give a man I'd loved so much.'

She knew the answer, but asked anyway. 'Does Ethan know all this?'

'No, I never had enough courage to tell him. Can you remember that I told you that I had to explain something to Ethan? I noticed that as Ethan got older he and Thomas didn't get on well but I thought it was just the usual kind of friction between adults and teenagers.

Thomas and he were so stiff and formal when they were together. Sometimes I wondered if Ethan had unearthed something, but I didn't have the courage to ask. I took the easy way out again, afraid to find out how Ethan would react.'

'Mrs Mason . . . '

'After all these years, it's about time you call me Susan.'

'Susan, it's important that you tell Ethan. I'm sure he'll understand. Why shouldn't he? He has a right to know.'

'Yes, yes, I realise that! I've often thought about it, especially since my stay in hospital. If I'd died, no-one would have known. I loved his father too much not to tell Ethan the truth.'

'There's probably never a right moment, is there? Why not just tell him next time you're sitting together. I'm sure Ethan will understand; probably better than you imagine.'

'Think so?'

'Yes! What about Ethan's relations? Are there any?'

'I don't think so. Ethan's father was an only child. I kept in touch with his parents until they died but they never knew about the baby, because I'm sure they'd have wanted to see Ethan. I didn't want to face Thomas's disapproval — and I'd also have needed to explain everything to Ethan. It was another wrong decision, and it's something else I regret. They died without knowing they had a grandson.'

'You must tell Ethan! Tell him all about his father; tell him about his real father's family. If he wants to find out more he will, but you must at least give him the chance.'

'Yes, I know you're right . . . I'm so glad I told you; it's such a relief to talk to someone about it after all these years. I hope Ethan understands and forgives me.'

'He will. Let's have some tea.' Lucy poured it into the delicate porcelain cups, and gave the older woman a chance to adjust.

'I have to go. I've promised to call

and see Colin, and I'm playing badminton with Pam later on. I'll come to see you again next time I'm home.'

'Please do.' Susan Mason looked more relaxed now and her face was calm again. She accompanied Lucy to the front door. 'I'll look forward to seeing you.'

Lucy couldn't resist. 'How's Ethan?'

'Fine! He's finishing the last bits of his book. He's gone down the village to get newspapers.' Susan Mason noticed Lucy's sad and wistful expression. The break-up had scarred her, and hurt Ethan too.

'Why did it go wrong Lucy?' She gave her a hug.

Lucy's eyes glistened. 'It's better that we found out before it was too late! Life never turns out exactly like you expect it to, does it?'

'Bye Lucy! Thanks for calling. Good luck in your new job, it sounds interesting.'

Lucy walked to her brother's house deep in thought. She took the back road, because she thought there was less chance of bumping into Ethan. She didn't want to meet him yet.

When he saw her, his step faltered for a second then he increased his pace again.

The wind was blowing his hair topsy-turvy. He wore a long black wool coat and a bright red scarf; it hung loosely round his neck. A couple of newspapers were tucked under his arm. At last they were face to face. She looked at him and tried to smile. 'Hello, Ethan. I've just come from your house.'

'How are you?' His eyes wandered hungrily over her face.

'Fine.'

'Good! I tried to write to you a couple of times, but I never managed to finish it.'

'Better so, I'd have had to reply. It's easier to get on with our lives, and be friends.'

The skin across his cheekbone was tight. 'Can we? Be friends, I mean?'

'I hope so, why not? It'll be a

different kind of friendship, but we ought to put what happened behind us and move on, don't you think?'

'Yes, you're right, although I don't deserve . . . '

She put up her hand to stop him. 'Please, Ethan. No reproaches, no regrets, no discussions.' To her own surprise she felt some of the bitterness fading.

He made a visible effort to change the subject too. 'Colin said you've started a new job. Tell me about it.'

She did, briefly, avoiding his glance. Her mouth was dry, and her pulse continued to race, but she hoped that she managed to sound normal.

'It sounds like a challenge; just right for you.'

'How's the book coming along?'

'Almost finished. I'm waiting for the editor's final approval.'

'What then? Back to Spain?' She watched every movement, every expression. She didn't need to commit anything to memory; his face, those eyes, everything about him was already firmly fixed in her head forever.

'Well, for a short visit perhaps. My agent has arranged a book tour for me. Not for this book, the previous one. You know the kind of thing — sitting in bookshops, and hoping that people are interested enough to buy a signed copy.'

He looked at her silently. She changed the subject quickly. 'I'm on my way to Colin's. I wanted to see Tim before he goes to bed.'

He nodded. 'I saw them the other day. He's a lovely kid. Colin and Judy are lucky.' He paused. 'Look after yourself.'

'You too.'

'Friends?' He put out his hand.

She placed hers, enclosed in soft woollen gloves, in his, and said, 'Friends.' She was glad she didn't need to feel his bare skin.

He managed a smile, and she withdrew her hand. She thrust it quickly into the pocket of her duffel coat. She had to get away. He still affected her in a way she hadn't thought possible.

★   ★   ★

Margaret and Lucy made good progress with the inventory of the books. Mr Walters visited them occasionally to check on various other things in the house. He often brought experts with him to value the furniture, china, glass, silver or other items. When he or other people stayed overnight, it livened things up.

On their own, Lucy and Margaret's evening's often comprised of reading, watching television or listening to music. Sometimes they went out to the local cinema or into Bath, and at the weekend both of them usually went home to their families.

Lucy had been concentrating on the computer screen when her attention was caught by someone wandering around the room. She watched him; he stopped here and there, taking a book out to examine it before putting it back again. Margaret was fetching coffee. Lucy was afraid that he'd mess up what they'd already achieved. 'Can I help you?'

He turned. He was a tall slim man with sandy hair and grey eyes. His face was thin with high cheekbones and good features and he had a light, healthy tan. He smiled as he walked leisurely towards her desk. 'I don't think so. I hope I'm not interrupting?'

'No, not as long as you put the books back exactly where you find them.'

'Ah! I take it that you're responsible for putting them into some kind of order?' He smiled and Lucy smiled back at him. 'I'm Andrew de Beer. And you're . . . ?'

'Lucy Waring. You're welcome to look at anything, as long as you put it back exactly where you find it, especially in the three sections at the end. We've finished those.'

'Who are 'we'?'

Lucy registered he had an unusual accent. It was soft and cultivated, but not one she immediately recognised. 'Margaret Ashton and me, we share the work.'

He glanced around the large room and smiled again. 'Quite a task for two people.'

'Are you looking for Mr Walters? I don't know if he's here; he wasn't this morning.'

'He is now; I came down with him from London.'

'What's your area?'

He looked puzzled. 'My area?'

'What area do you specialise in, furniture, jewellery, glass?'

The laughter lines deepened. 'I specialise in investment. Haven't the foggiest clue about all of this.' His hands made vague sweeping movements. Lucy was curious, but thought it better not to ask questions. She turned back to the computer. He liked the way she reacted; he liked the way she looked too.

Mr Walters hurried into the room. 'Ah, there you are. I've found the chest of drawers I was telling you about, it's a fantastic piece of furniture in perfect condition. If you take my advice you'll put it on your listing. Morning, Lucy! How are you? You've met Sir Andrew?'

Lucy looked up, her mouth opened to say something, but then she snapped it shut.

'Oh, Henry, please! I wish you'd forget the 'Sir' bit.'

'It's your title. Even if you don't like it; you're still Sir Andrew de Beer.'

He laughed softly. 'I don't suppose I'll use it very much once I'm back in Nassau, although on the other hand it might impress my American clients. Americans love titles.'

'Come on, my dear chap, I want to show you the most beautiful pieces personally. They're spread all over the place. See you later, Lucy!'

Andrew de Beer lifted his hand in a parting gesture and trailed after Mr Walters.

Lucy told Margaret about the visitor, and her eyes lit up. 'How exciting! The house has been in the de Beer family for centuries; the last direct descendant died leaving only a distant relative, that must be the de Beer you just met. The house and grounds have to be auctioned because of death duties. Pity, isn't it?' she grinned. 'We'll have to dress up for supper!'

9

Andrew De Beer was an interesting dinner companion and Mr Walters' dry wit made it a very pleasant meal.

Next morning Lucy met Andrew in the garden, as she was about to drive to Bath. She told him where she was going and he said he'd like to see the town. Out of politeness she offered him a lift. To her surprise, he accepted. On the way he told her how he'd left London to find a more exciting life in America. From there he'd drifted to the Bahamas. He described his home in Nassau. It sounded like a wonderful place to live. They arranged to meet later for coffee and she went off to do her shopping.

When they got back to the house he asked her to help him choose a couple of items to keep. The temptation was too great; she postponed her trip home. They went from room to room on the

146

ground floor and they picked out a pair of lacquered Chinese tallboys, some landscape paintings and a fantastic mahogany sideboard. She stayed and they shared the evening meal and a bottle of dry white wine.

Lucy relaxed and enjoyed his company; he was polite, undemanding and interesting. Next morning, after breakfast, he asked her to help him to look around the first floor and the nursery. Lucy admired lots of things, the house was a veritable treasure chest, but he only added an elegant lady's writing desk and a highly-polished cherrywood dressing table to his list. He explained that his home was too small to take many pieces and selling things was more important than owning them. The house and its contents held no personal associations. It was more sensible to let it go to auction, to pay off the death duties. If he were lucky there'd be some money left over for him.

'The day is young,' she said impulsively. 'Would you like to come home with me? I'm sure my parents would like to meet you, there's always room for one more at our table.'

'Are you sure?'

'Certain; or perhaps you'd rather spend the day here?'

He shook his head. 'I'd rather come with you.'

'Right, I'll just tell the housekeeper not to expect us for anymore meals today. She'll be glad to have us out of the way for a bit I expect.'

He smiled. 'Right! I'll put this list in my room, get my coat and meet you by your car.'

He was polite and charming. He complemented her mother on the meal. She didn't know very much about him, but he was at ease with them all, and pleasant company. She wondered what her parents thought. Lucy noticed how her mother eyed him speculatively, but Mrs Waring didn't ask too many personal questions, and she didn't quiz Lucy about him either when they were on their own. Time passed quickly.

On the way back, he said, 'I like your parents. They're nice people.'

'Yes, I like them too. They have a philosophical attitude to life; especially my dad.'

'Very sensible; you have to make the best of things, and hope for your share of luck.'

Getting ready for bed, Lucy felt more relaxed than for several weeks. She knew it was because Andrew had filled a little of the emptiness she'd felt since Christmas. She'd been forced to push Ethan into the background for once.

Before leaving, Andrew asked Lucy to come up to London for a weekend. Lucy agreed. She needed to move on and meet other people. She continued to dream about Ethan, but it was nice to know other men like Andrew were interested in her company, even if he wasn't.

The days were beginning to lengthen at last. It was pleasant to walk through the extensive parkland after work. There were fat buds on ancient trees now, and the first patches of bright daffodils were spread out below their wide branches.

She made a flying visit home at the end of the week, to pick up some clothes. Helping Lucy to park, her mother knew there was no point in hanging on to the wish that Lucy and Ethan would get back together. Lucy deserved happiness, if not with Ethan, then perhaps with someone else. 'Enjoy yourself. He is a nice chap; no snobbery or false airs and graces.'

'Yes, I like him too.'

Mrs Waring was glad to see her daughter smiling again. She'd lost weight and had developed shadows under her eyes since she and Ethan had broken their engagement.

Andrew was a perfect companion. In fact, the whole weekend turned out well. He wasn't Ethan, but he aimed to please her. Lucy tried not to compare the two of them; it wasn't easy. They wandered around London on Saturday looking at the tourist attractions, and in the evening they went to see a musical.

Lucy enjoyed it.

They had a final glass of wine in a bar after the theatre, and when he kissed her in the lift on the way to their rooms she didn't resist, but registered no excitement, and no thrill.

She willed herself to forget Ethan but it wasn't that simple. The memories of how she'd fallen apart in Ethan's arms still made her hunger for him and no one else could replace him. They parted amiably and smiling at each other; their rooms were in opposite directions.

Next day after sharing lunch together, Andrew took her to the station.

'I wish you worked in London. I enjoyed the weekend very much.'

Lucy nodded. 'Yes. So did I. Thank you for everything.'

Andrew nodded. 'A pleasure! I'll ring you tomorrow.'

He stood and waved from the barrier as she boarded the train.

He did phone next day. By the time Lucy put down the phone, they'd agreed he'd come down again the following weekend. Lucy was flattered.

They visited the pub on Friday. On Saturday, after a leisurely breakfast Lucy suggested they visited a nearby stately home. They did, but didn't go inside.

Andrew protested loudly, 'There are plenty of antiques and history in my uncle's place; I want to enjoy the present. Let's just walk through the park. He told her about his home, about his friends, and she chatted about anything that popped into her head, apart from Ethan. That evening they had a cosy meal in a small country restaurant. He was attentive, very attentive, but he wasn't Ethan.

Sunday morning he surprised her by saying he wanted to visit the local churchyard. They walked to the village and wandered through the graveyard looking for family tombs. He draped his arm around her shoulder as they stood and tried to read inscriptions. She didn't resist, although the gesture reminded her of Ethan. She wondered how long Ethan would haunt her life. How long would he block a new beginning? They lunched at the village pub and Lucy vowed to push the memories of meals with Ethan in Spain to the back of her mind. She noticed he was toying with his wine.

'I know this is rushing you, but lots of time is the one thing I don't have at the moment. I can't put off my journey home much longer. Will you come with me?'

She caught her breath. 'You're joking; you can't mean it? We hardly know each other.'

'I know all I need to know about you. I've never liked anyone so much or so fast before, and I know I don't want us to say goodbye. It's enough for me!'

'I can't just follow you across the Atlantic!'

'Why not? You told me you have no special boyfriend here and your job in the house ends in a couple of weeks doesn't it? Have you got another job lined up yet?'

'No. Margaret knows someone who thinks they can find us work in London.'

'I can find you work; I've contacts all over the island.'

Lucy was flabbergasted; her expression spoke bands.

'I know this comes as a bit of a surprise, but think about it seriously, Lucy.'

She was staring at him bemused; her mouth was slightly open. He touched her cheek and she had to stop herself turning away from him. Ethan had done the same; so often! 'I'll think about it.'

He looked pleased. 'At least you haven't turned me down on the spot — that gives me a little hope. I'm sure that you'd love the Bahamas; it really is paradise. It's only a couple of hours' flight from your friends and family too.' He smiled, and she couldn't help smiling too.

She did think about it. There was nothing to hold her back, but something did. Lucy went home the following weekend and told her mother about Andrew's offer.

Mrs Waring didn't want Lucy to go, but she was clever enough not to interfere or to try to influence her daughter. 'It's up to you, love.'

'It's tempting, but I'm trying to be sensible. I hardly know him.'

Her mother nodded. 'Take your time about it. Be absolutely sure.'

She went to see Colin and Judy that afternoon. She was about to ring the bell when the door opened and her brother stood in the doorway with Tim in the pushchair. 'Hi sis! I'm going for a walk with this little devil. Judy's gone to see her grandmother in hospital. Coming?'

'Yes, of course.' They strolled leisurely along the back road that ran parallel with the river. It was cool but the fresh air was reviving. 'How are things?' she asked.

'Good. Very busy in work at the moment, but I prefer it that way.'

Lucy nodded. 'You're a bit of a

workaholic. You should start your own business!' He surprised her.

'I will one day. It's always been at the back of my mind.'

She smiled. 'I'm sure you'd make a success of it.'

He paused. 'Did Judy tell you that Ethan has offered to lend us his villa for a couple of weeks in the summer?'

She looked across towards the river. 'No; that's kind of him. I'm sure you'd like it. It's off the beaten track, but it isn't far to the coast, and there are lots of places to visit nearby.'

'You won't mind if we accept? If it makes things difficult for you . . . you know that you always have my first loyalty.'

She kissed him quickly on his cheek. 'Thanks! That's sweet! Don't worry; it's fine with me, promise! Ethan and I have agreed to stay friends.'

'Really?' He looked relieved.

'It's our mistake, not yours. It has nothing to do with your friendship. I don't mind at all, honestly. In fact I'd feel bad if I knew I'd come between you two.'

He was silent for a moment. 'It was a pity it didn't work out.'

She sighed. 'These things happen. You've seen him recently?'

'He spends more time in the village now. We went to the pub for a beer last night, just Ethan and I. It was like old times. Judy said she didn't mind.'

'Did you? How is he?'

'He never drinks much, never did, but last night he drank too much, too fast. He talked a lot of confused rubbish.'

'What do you mean . . . rubbish?'

'He's sure I'd never abuse his trust, that's why he probably mentioned her to me . . . some woman he's met.'

Lucy breathed deeply, tried not to appear too interested.

Colin continued. 'I don't know who he was talking about because it all came out in tangled phrases and I didn't want to stop him because I had the feeling he needed to get it off his chest. When he said 'she's been hurt once, doesn't deserve to be hurt again — she deserves to be happy', I wondered if he was talking about that lawyer. That woman, Rachael, is divorced isn't she? I can't imagine who else he could mean, can you?'

It took Lucy a big effort to reply. She had to steady her voice. 'No. I think she's always been interested in him and perhaps it's now a mutual interest.'

'She's all right, I suppose; attractive to look at, but she's a career type, and ambitious. He used to like uncomplicated girls, but perhaps his taste has changed over the years.'

'Now that you are real friends again, he'll be sure to tell you if anything special is in the air. So, are you going to Spain?'

Colin answered and Lucy listened with one ear; glad that she didn't have to contribute much to the conversation. The information about Ethan and Rachael had punched a hole in her heart.

She went to see Mrs Mason on Sunday morning. She thought Ethan might be working on the book, or even sleeping late. His mother opened the door and Lucy followed her to the living room. 'It's lovely to see you! I'll get some tea. Look who's here, Ethan?'

With a knot in her throat, Lucy barely had time to adjust before Mrs Mason turned away and left them alone. Her pulse escalated; there was a fluttering inside her stomach like a frantic butterfly, and she couldn't control the excitement. It would never change. 'H . . . hello Ethan. How are things?' She thought that he looked tired.

'Fine! I've sent the final version of the book to the publisher at last.'

She felt strangely tongue-tied. Something between them had changed forever; she'd never felt lost for words before and she noticed he wasn't very talkative either.

Mrs Mason came in with a laden tea tray. 'I've told Ethan about his father,

Lucy. He guessed there was something hidden in the past, so it was a relief for him to know the truth.'

Ethan looked at his mother in surprise. 'Lucy already knows?'

'It slipped out one day when she was here. She told me to tell you, and I did.'

Lucy looked at him and found his nearness overwhelming. He made her senses reel. 'Your mother said it's bothered her for years, so the truth was the best thing for you both.'

He nodded. It doesn't change any-thing, but it straightens out the wrinkles.' He smiled softly. 'It wasn't easy for her. My relationship with my step-father would have been better too, if we'd always been honest with each other.'

Lucy turned to his mother. 'I told you he'd understand, didn't I, Susan?'

'Yes, I should have explained things a long time ago.'

Mrs Mason handed her a cup of coffee. 'Still in Bath?'

'Yes, but it's coming to an end.'

'And then? Your mother told me you might be going to the Bahamas. Your mum mentioned that you met someone in Bath who comes from there.'

Lucy reddened. 'I haven't decided yet. This chap is going back to Nassau soon, and he invited me to go along. He says he'll find me a job, but I may look for a job in London.' Lucy noticed how Ethan picked up his cup and walked to the window recess.

'When will you finish in Bath?'

'Most of the listing work is finished; we're tying up the loose ends now.'

Ethan turned, put the cup back into the saucer again, it rattled as he did so. He shoved his hands into his pockets and hunched his shoulders. 'The Bahamas? That's exotic.'

Susan Mason said, 'Things are certainly moving for you now, aren't they? Bath, then London or the Bahamas! I hope it all works out.'

'Thanks!' Lucy changed the subject. 'Mum said you're all busy making things for the summer bazaar.' They chatted for a while and Lucy noticed Ethan was silent, and staring out of the window. She wondered if she made him feel uncomfortable. She got up. 'I'll be off.'

'Don't forget to write and send me a postcard from the Caribbean!'

'If I go.'

Mrs Mason got up.

'It's all right, Mum, I'll see Lucy to the door.'

Lucy followed him down the short passageway. 'So long, Ethan.'

'Bye Lucy! Take care of yourself.'

'You too!' Staring up at his face, there was a blank expression in his eyes. She longed to touch him, but of course she didn't. She wished she could think of something clever to say. She threw back her shoulders and kept on walking. When she reached the gates, she looked back; he was still standing. She waved, and he lifted his hand before he went indoors.

The end of the following week, she travelled up to London to see Andrew.

She'd thought a lot about his offer. She liked him and the chance to see the Bahamas was tempting, but that wasn't enough. She realised the decision had never really been in doubt and wanted to tell him personally. He knew that he'd be travelling alone when he saw the expression in her eyes when they met. She was an honest person. He knew that she wouldn't want to intentionally hurt him.

'You're not coming are you?'

'No. Please don't be angry. It wouldn't work.'

'I'm not angry, just a little sad. I really hoped you'd say yes. Perhaps it was just the wrong moment? The invitation stands. You've my address. Any time you change your mind!'

Lucy leaned forward and kissed him gently on his lips. 'Thanks for being so nice to me. I wish you happiness. I wish you love. Have a safe flight and take care of yourself.' She got up and turned to go, there was no point in dragging things out.

He watched her for a moment before he remembered something. 'Lucy, wait! I don't know why, probably because you clearly weren't keen from the word go, but I'd the feeling you wouldn't come. Here is a parting gift from me!' He handed her a shoebox-size package.

On the train, during the homeward journey she stared at the countryside and wondered why life sometimes pushed the wrong people together. She only remembered the parcel lying unopened on her lap much later. She found it contained an old porcelain doll she'd fallen in love with when they inspected the nursery together at the house. It was thoughtful of him; a parting gift that was quite unique; something that would always remind her of him.

10

The last few weeks in Bath passed quickly; they double-checked for mistakes. They started to think about finding new jobs. Margaret was visiting her sister at the weekend, and intended to study the situation vacant columns in the London papers. Lucy wasn't too worried; her bank account was healthy and something would turn up. At home her mother mentioned that she'd heard that Ethan had gone back to Spain. Lucy wasn't brave enough to ask her mother if Ethan and Rachael's names were linked or even if Rachael had gone back with him.

She offered to do some weekend shopping, and met Susan Mason in the High Street. 'I must say, you're looking tip-top at last. Your chest infection is clearly a thing of the past!'

'I feel really well, Lucy! This kind of weather helps.'

'Yes, it's much warmer isn't it? Mum said Ethan's gone back to Spain? Miss him?'

'Yes, I do, but he was so nervous and jumpy before he left. He insisted everything was all right and he sounds a little better on the phone, but I can never be sure when I can't see his face. He's helping Antonio with trellis-work, whatever that means; perhaps it's having a steadying effect.'

'He's probably still winding down after finishing the last book.'

'Perhaps! How are you? Were your ears burning recently, your mum and I were talking about you. She told me you're not going to the Bahamas after all; I think she was relieved. So what happens now?'

'I don't know yet.'

'Your mother said he was a nice fellow.'

'He was, but no-one special.'

She nodded and patted Lucy's hand. 'Then you made the right decision.'

'I don't want to go too far, in case an

interview turns up out of the blue. I'm hoping for some sun though. When I went to the travel agent's there was a poster of Looe on the wall. I went there on holiday with Mum and Dad once years ago when I was small, and I always wanted to go back. Pam was going to come with me, but then she started to think about the expense of her wedding in September and has decided not to after all. I don't mind, it's lovely weather for walking, and if it stays like this it'll be great. I've already booked a couple of days from the 15th till the 19th.'

'It's beautiful thereabouts. Ethan's grandparents are buried in a small churchyard in a tiny village not far from Looe. I've visited their grave once or twice since they died to tidy the grave, but it's not easy to get there without a car. Perhaps Ethan will take it over for me now.'

'I'll go there, if you like.'

'Would you? That would be kind.'

'It'll give me somewhere definite to

aim for when I'm walking. Where is it exactly?'

'Call in on your way back. I'll give you the details.'

'Right!' She glanced at her watch. 'Gosh, I'd better get a move on, I promised Mum to be back with the shopping by twelve. She wants the cabbage for lunch.'

'She's making sure you have some decent food, eh?'

Lucy smiled. 'How did you guess?'

'Cos I'm the same with Ethan.' It was on the tip of Mrs Mason's tongue to comment that Lucy looked tired, but she didn't.

'Give Ethan my best wishes.' Lucy was glad she could mention his name so casually. She didn't want to mention Rachael, and Mrs Mason hadn't either — perhaps she didn't want to hurt Lucy's feelings by referring to a new girlfriend in Ethan's life.

'I will, next time I talk to him!'

★ ★ ★

The weather was lovely. She'd arrived two days ago. The hotel was comfortable and there weren't many other visitors so early in the year. Lucy enjoyed the peace and already felt more relaxed than she had for weeks. She was even sleeping better. Walking for most of yesterday had tired her physically and also made her muscles ache.

Today after a good breakfast she drove several miles down the coast and parked her car in an empty parking lot off the main road. She checked the map, folded it, and put it into her backpack. She set out to follow the cliff path that led to the small fishing village where Ethan's grandparents were buried.

Lucy's thoughts circled too. She knew there was no easy solution, no easy way to forget Ethan, but her granddad had an old saying 'There's an ointment that heals all wounds — the ointment of time.' Lucy hoped he was right. When she reached the picturesque fishing village with its narrow cobbled streets and small asymmetric houses, there wasn't even a café. The small pub was closed but it would be open when she came back. She had to find the graveyard first. There wasn't a flower shop either, but the owner of the grocery shop told her there were usually bunches of flowers for sale at the petrol station on the road leading down to the small harbour.

Lucy bought a bunch of daffodils and followed the main road leading inland. It branched off at the top of the hill, and she followed the narrow lane meandering its way to the local church.

The church itself was locked, and most of the gravestones in the grave-yard were weathered and covered in moss and lichen. Lucy followed Mrs Mason's directions and had no trouble finding the right grave. It was close to a boundary wall. She was surprised to discover fresh narcissi in a black marble pot, and that someone else had already tidied the grave. Perhaps there were other living relatives nearby after all?

She arranged her flowers in a jam jar

she found behind the headstone, and stood for a couple of minutes watching the yellow daffodils moving in the wind. She thought about the unknown couple named Henry and Annie Osmann — Ethan's grandparents. She turned away, threading her way through the headstones towards the lychgate. Closing it quietly behind her, she started on her return journey to the village.

She'd almost reached the end of the lane when she saw a man coming towards her. Her breath caught in her throat; it was Ethan. Her thoughts were turmoil; Lucy stopped and waited until he came closer . . . 'Ethan! What are you doing here?'

'My mother told me you were coming here. I've been hanging around waiting for you.'

'Why? Is something wrong?' She took a deep breath. She still hadn't absorbed the shock of finding him so unexpectedly in this quiet place.

'I had to talk to you. I couldn't wait

any longer.' His breath was ragged.

Lucy swallowed the lump in her throat. Thrown off-balance she didn't know what to answer, so she waited and time seemed to stand still.

'I scuttled back to Spain because I thought you'd be going to the Bahamas.'

She shook her head; stifled the feeling of delight because he was so close. She forced herself to answer casually. 'No.'

Lucy stared at him, mesmerised. She knew she was being foolish and needed to calm down. She forced herself to concentrate on the leaves rustling in the wind and the warmth of the sun on her face but it didn't help — she could only think that it really was Ethan standing in front of her. Her glance was drawn irrevocably to his face and she drowned in the effect his eyes had on her soul.

She registered the faint perfume of sandalwood on his skin and the solidity of his body. She felt as if she had no will of her own. The desire to reach out and touch him was overwhelming; she hoped he couldn't read her thoughts. His voice dragged her attention back to earth again.

'Why not? I thought you were in love with him?'

'Who told you that? I like him, but there's a difference between liking and loving.'

There was a moment of silence. 'Poor devil!' His expression softened and his voice sounded gentle. His hands cupped her face and one of his thumbs rubbed its way gently across her lower lip.

'Don't Ethan.' She turned her face away, the backpack in her hand slid to the ground. Her voice caught in her throat and it was an effort to say. 'Don't fool around with me, save that kind of thing for Rachael.'

He looked puzzled. 'Rachael? What on earth has Rachael got to do with it?'

'I don't want complications in my life. Colin told me about you two.'

'Colin told you about who? Me and Rachael?' He still looked bewildered.

'You . . . you were down the pub with Colin a while back . . . and you talked to him about someone who'd been hurt badly once, and deserved something better.'

She watched and waited. There was still no comprehension or understanding on his face.

She stumbled on. 'Rachael is divorced. Colin thought you were talking about her, that you were in love with her.'

For a moment he didn't make heads or tails of what she was saying, but then he looked at her with amusement before he shook his head and smiled. 'Oh, Lucy. What a mix-up. Rachael is my legal adviser, nothing more. I haven't seen her for weeks. I remember vaguely rambling on at Colin once down the pub, but I'm sure if I was talking about anyone, it was you!'

Her expression was one of slight amazement.

He shifted position and looked hesitant. 'I'm sure that I love you! I didn't know what the words meant until I'd spent time with you and fell in love without knowing it. I followed you here because as soon as I heard you hadn't gone to the Bahamas I had to see you. I have to tell you how much I love you, and hope that you'll give me another chance.'

Lucy wondered if she was dreaming. 'A chance? You mean a chance for us?'

He reached out and pulled her towards him. 'I've never wanted anyone like this before. I know now that you're the only woman I want, and the only one I'll ever need. I knew it before the plane took off, that day, in Spain. I realised I'd lost the most important person in my life. It was too late for me to put things right because you were already out of reach.'

Lucy caught her breath. With a mounting excitement she said, 'But . . . what about all your talk about independence?' There was a knot in her stomach. 'This isn't a joke, is it?'

He held her in his arms and she could look into his eyes. She could see it was no joke. Lucy felt how all the aching unhappiness of the past weeks slid away as their lips met. Both of them knew that the confusion and heartbreak was behind them. The magic began to work again. 'I've dreamt of this moment for so long. I can't believe it's really happening.'

His hands framed her face. 'Now that things are coming right at last, I'm tempted to say I think you were born for me. I've never felt anything like that before! You give me a reason to live.' She smiled. 'I know I don't deserve it, but forgive me and give me another chance, Lucy! Tell me you care for me a little, please.'

She swallowed and said quietly. 'I've always been yours, Ethan, as long as I can remember. That's why it hurt so much to lose you in Spain like that.'

Released from the torment of the picture of her in the arms of another man, the black icicles tobogganed off his soul and melted away in the sunshine of her smile. She said she was his, but even now he could hardly believe it.

Lucy touched his face. 'I've always loved you and always will.' Her breathing was fast.

Ethan lifted her off her feet. 'Marry me? As soon as possible?' The smile in his eyes was sensuous.

She met his smile and her eyes sparkled. 'I will, if you really want me.'

'If I want you? I'm prepared to put it down in black and white, in letters six feet high if you like. I have to go on that book tour, but we could marry after that, in six weeks' time?'

'You make it sound so simple!'

'It is. You know me; I'm not one for much fuss.' He hastened to add, 'But perhaps you want an elaborate affair?'

'I don't care, but I think our families won't let us get away with something simple.'

'Hmm! You're right — especially after what happened. They'll expect the complete works! All right, I can cope with it if it makes everyone happy. I'll be the happiest one there anyway, whatever we decide to do!'

'And after that? Do I just sit around all day in Spain and warm your slippers?'

He grinned. 'No, I can't imagine you doing that for long. What would you like to do? Would you like me to move back home permanently?'

'Would you?'

He paused, but only for a second. 'If that's what you want. I could do without a lot of things but you are not one of them, not anymore.'

Lucy felt euphoric. He loved her; she'd never been so sure. 'I know how much you love Spain and it's a perfect place for your writing, but I need to do something too!'

'Hmm! You can learn Spanish: there's a retired teacher in the village. He taught me.'

'And the rest of the week?' she said, tilting her head and wrinkling her nose.

'How about the Growers' Association? It'd give you a little regular employment and take some of the pressure off me. I used to toy with the idea of organising tours to the vineyards from the Costa Brava. How about you organising something like that?'

'You mean wine-tasting tours?'

'Yes, and perhaps including a visit to our taverna for some local fare.'

'Tit-bits to eat, wine-tasting followed by wine sale? Right, why not.' He chuckled and her eyes sparkled. 'We could display your paintings, local arts and crafts and sell them.'

'You could teach English to foreigners. There are enough people in the vicinity who would be glad of one-to-one instruction.' Lucy nodded. He studied her, his face full of fun. 'And not forgetting . . . the house is ideal for children — our children.'

She felt quite heady. The idea of their children, Ethan's and hers, was breathtaking.

Ethan grabbed her and pulled her to him; her feet left the ground. 'I've never honestly thought about children before, but it's a wonderful idea. A couple like Tim would be fun.'

Lucy's happiness bubbled again. 'A couple?'

He laughed and it glided into a throaty chuckle. He swung her around in a gentle circle, his voice rung with happiness. 'And I want some attention too.'

Lucy felt awestruck. 'You'll always be my first and last priority.' Her face was on level with his; she revelled in the laughter in the depths of those blue eyes.

THE END

SEE NO EVIL

Patricia Robins

Evelyn, Gay and Margaret are sisters. When their widowed mother dies, the caring Evelyn is thrust into looking after Margaret, who was born blind. Gay, always pursuing her own interests, is happy to be taken out by the rich Gordon de Verriland, leaving Evelyn wondering if she will ever meet someone herself. Then, when Nicky March comes into Evelyn's life, could he be the one for her? Or will Gay's own interests ruin her hope of love?

INTRUDER IN PARADISE

Stella Kent

Selena Brent had been Miss Hallows' companion for two years, and she treasured Cloudhallows as though it belonged to her. Unfortunately, when Miss Hallows died, it was beyond Selena's pocket, and she could only wonder who would buy the house. She was convinced it would be a brash, insensitive type who would want the lovely old building modernised and dragged into the twentieth-century. But that was just the first wrong conclusion she was to make about Mark Denning . . .

WINDS OF CHANGE

Fay Wentworth

When Kate returns to Stony Ridge Farm, she doesn't expect to find a strange man living in her cottage. Who is Grant and why is he there? Her parents trust him, but a mysterious visitor arouses Kate's suspicions. What has happened to divide the farming community and cause conflict between friends? She determines to discover the truth. As secrets from the past cause turmoil in the present, Kate finds herself questioning her own feelings . . .

COMING HOME

Susan Sarapuk

When Maddy Green, new vicar of Llyn Ddu, meets the land-owning Collett-Evans family she falls for charming Tristan and dislikes sullen Ben. But all is not as it seems. As Maddy battles opposition in the parish and tries to help troubled teenager Chloe, secrets are revealed leading to the downfall of one brother and the redemption of another, a suicide attempt and breaking of a curse. Ultimately, will Maddy find love and a place to belong?

OUT OF REACH

Beth James

Carolyn, never having seen her real father, decides to track him down, although she's devastated that her boyfriend, Andy, is against the scheme. Nevertheless, she sets out alone to Australia, meeting the attractive Nick Packer en route. Soon her quest to find her father seems impossible. Far from her home and family, her relationship with Andy becomes increasingly frosty, whilst her ripening friendship with Nick suddenly seems so very tempting . . . Caroline has some serious choices to make.